A Pitying
of Doves

A Pitying of Doves

Felicity McCall

eve

Published in May 2011

eve is an imprint of Guildhall Press dedicated to encouraging, promoting and showcasing the creativity of women authors and artists.

Guildhall Press
Unit 15, Ráth Mór Business Park
Bligh's Lane, Derry
Ireland
BT48 0LZ
(028) 7136 4413
info@ghpress.com
www.ghpress.com

 Guildhall Press gratefully acknowledges the financial support of the Arts Council of Northern Ireland as a principal funder under its Annual Support for Organisations Programme.

The author asserts her moral rights in this work in accordance with the Copyright, Designs and Patents Act 1998.

Copyright © Guildhall Press/Felicity McCall
ISBN: 978 1 906271 35 0

A CIP record for this book is available from the British Library.

Acknowledgements

My thanks and gratitude to: the Arts Council of Northern Ireland and its Literature Officer, Damian Smyth, for support and inspiration; Paul Hippsley, Declan Carlin, Jenni Doherty, Joe McAllister, Kevin Hippsley and all at Guildhall Press for incomparable standards of professional guidance and excellence; my fellow writers, theatre practitioners and artists/activists whose constructive criticism, cynical good humour and boundless energy sustains me through the writing process; all my loved ones, for your generosity of spirit and faith . . . you know who you are, I know how special you make my life.

And central among you, Aoife, always.

For Mary, Oonagh, Debbie, Geraldine, Kevin, Jim and everyone who shared being young. And who told me that one day I would write.

Also Dr David and the late Rev Bill and Fr Kevin, who helped to open the door to the future.

The Author

A BBC staff journalist for twenty years of the NI conflict, Felicity McCall began the millennium as a full-time writer as well as an occasional broadcaster, arts facilitator and actor. *A Pitying of Doves* is her twelfth publication. Her titles include fiction, non-fiction, plays and a graphic novel and she has contributed to three anthologies. The co-founder and director of two theatre companies, Felicity has had twelve plays staged professionally and four screenplay credits. Her awards include the Tyrone Guthrie for stage and screenplay, and several ACNI SIAP awards; her nominations include two Meyer Whitworth and two IPSG for best new play.

Derry City Council's 2011 'Woman of the Year for the Arts,' her forthcoming schedule includes appearances at literary festivals, the publication of her first teenage novel and a documentary screenplay. While her work will be performed, read and screened in Europe, the US and Australasia, she continues to live and write in Derry and Donegal.

Felicity is also the Ireland officer for the miscarriage of justice lobby group, Portia. She has an adult daughter, Aoife.

Introduction

A Pitying of Doves is based round the common theme of the people of a purpose-built border mill village and how they cope after the mill, which was their very reason for living there, has closed down. It is *of* the conflict but not *about* it. In these stories, I hope to reflect the symbiotic relationship between a people and an environment and to explore how the circumstances of time and place may define our life far more than external politics.

The period and the setting of this collection mean there is, inevitably, an element of memoir in the mood and atmosphere. It is, however, a work of fiction.

Foreword

Probably the only annoying thing about a book is that there are often a few pages devoted at the outset to someone telling the reader what it's about, what to look out for, where the good bits are, what it all means and how wise they were by doing what they have already done – acquiring it in the first place.

Heaven forbid my comments are as irritating.

Having been long aware of the author's achievements as a writer, my remarks should be no more than a kind of welcome mat inside the front door of the cover. Felicity McCall needs no assistance in engaging and holding anyone's attention.

Her passion for storytelling takes many forms, from radio to stage drama, children's writing to short fiction, screenplays and full-length fiction. The consistency of artistic delivery across those media has successfully tested the capacity of her themes to be compelling and fruitful.

I think I can say that this collection of short fiction acts as something of a 'McCall Reader', gathering in many of the threads of her other work, the fabric of her imaginative world. She is an 'occupied' writer – landscape, allegiance, memory, place, time (with its distinctive markers of fashion and habit), repel and compel her by turns; but she also reflects on a common, shared culture riven by disquiet and hurt, both public and secret, not always dramatic or conventionally remarkable.

Among her characters here, growing in familiarity from story to story, are other, dislocated, un-rooted, memorable figures, both haunted and haunting. Francie, in *Paddy Tohill and The SAS*, tobacco in one pocket, a tin of dog food in the other; the elderly bachelor killed by a booby-trapped men's magazine in *The Grip of Winter*; Cissie, in *Lace Gloves and Quiet Desperation*, "hunched on the top step, weeping silently, too dignified to look for pity"; and Evie, as close to a narrator as the collection comes, a life behind her in the metropolitan glamour of London, recognising the threat and comfort of a future alone among the "dark sentinel yew trees" of home in the story which gives the book its title. Characters such as these patrol the stories with an unnerving coincidence, strange casualties of the forces which propel childish gangs and adult passions to closure of a sort.

But readers should not prepare themselves for a grim and melancholy read in the manner of so much 'Troubles' fiction. The stories here are contemporary in their handling of the complex loyalties of her chosen ground. In a work like *A Mother's Love*, they quietly reinforce those qualities of character which so often go unregistered in fiction generally, let alone in fiction from Northern Ireland – reticence, silence, selflessness.

Yes, the narratives unfurl against a backdrop of vexation and dismay but most of those take place within simple lives simply led. The 'SAS' of one story is no more tangible or real or 'come across' than – but every bit as exotic and fictional as would be – the Yeti. And among the many remarkable features of London, the 'big city', is the plausible and everyday observation, for a young girl from rural Ulster – where every young man 'was' – that "every young man with an English accent was not a British soldier". The events of several lifetimes flick through joy, excitement, misperceptions, mystery and loss, and if there is desperation occasionally, there is not despair.

For all her passion for detail, and the complexities of her themes – there is no easy pigeon-holing of sheep and goats in her narratives of community – McCall's eye is refreshingly dispassionate and cooly humane. Perhaps this is something of a legacy of her career as a journalist and broadcaster. Perhaps it is an echo of her 'political' commitment to lost causes, miscarriages of justice, the forgotten and sometimes despised.

Wherever it comes from, it makes for a gentle style – something like that "soft purity" Evie notes in the countryside – where love and displacement, joy and injury, brutality and the unexpected, the meditative and the untrammelled, are described for the record and for good.

Welcome in.

Damian Smyth
Damian Smyth is a poet and writer. He is Head of Literature and Drama with the Arts Council of Northern Ireland.

Contents

The stories are in chronological order but may be read independently of each other.

The Cardinal Conway Essay Prize

THE RELATIONSHIP BETWEEN MARY O'CAROLAN AND Father Magee could best be described as challenging and they usually maintained an uneasy peace. There was a mutual recognition of each other's position in society, an acceptance of due deference and the common ground of the spiritual welfare of all but a handful of the Primary 4, 5 and 6 children at the village school. Aside from that, Father Magee's generosity of spirit prevented it becoming anything other than courteous. But the pupils knew that should Mrs O'Carolan be in the grip of one of her particularly virulent bouts of the aggressive frustration that had once been directed at the now-absent Mr O'Carolan, Father Magee would intercede on their behalf and lead them outside for a game of football. So on Friday, at least, the class had some sort of protection from the vitriolic whippet of a woman who could lash into their hands, legs, backs and heads with the strength of a man twice her size, and often for no reason other than her grievance against life in general and men in particular.

In truth, Mrs O'Carolan doubted whether rumbustious games of mixed-sex football were the best way to foster cross-community relations, but Father Magee assured her that young people who learned to play together in a spirit of healthy competition were being imbued with positive Christian values. Mrs O'Carolan wondered whether he had ever fallen victim to one of Frankie Tohill's sliding tackles, for she had often occasion to bandage the resulting skinned ankles and pierced insteps, and there was nothing very Christian about them.

But the arrival of the priest on his vintage Vespa invariably elicited shouts and cheers from Catholic, Anglican and Nonconformist alike, so she knew she was fighting a losing battle against a groundswell of ecumenical fervour. That and genuine and heartfelt affection. Mrs O'Carolan found this difficult to comprehend. In her world, adults ruled by fear and domination. And she would never forgive the man, priest of God though he was, for failing to suppress his laughter when she had asked him the perfectly pertinent theological question: what religion were Adam and Eve?

Some of the non-Catholics were too quick to lay claim to everything, she felt, like Evie Millar's family professing to be Holy Catholics, with their prayers of St John Chrysostom and veritable lexicon of saints, their Lenten observations and their frankly superior knowledge of the Gospels. She was more at home with Dissenters, like the strange young lad McClintock from the hill farm who had been born of too old a mother and seemed to have difficulty relating to any aspect of the school curriculum – secular or spiritual. He was happiest when sitting quietly, playing with the broken alarm clock that he carried everywhere.

In addition, she had inherited with her latest Primary 4s two firebrand cousins whose families subscribed to some sort of ascetic sect that embraced three separate acts of worship on a Sunday and which forbade them to read, knit or eat hot food on the Lord's Day. At some subliminal level, she felt it was her duty to bring them to the One True Faith but accepted leaving this responsibility to Father Magee. If only he would leave matters of discipline in her hands, things could be much more satisfactory. However, her class knew that she could easily be redirected from potentially violent incursions into mathematics, spelling and the capital cities of the world by the most inane questions that touched on the vast grey area blanketing Christianity and Celtic, even pagan, folklore.

* * * *

By the time she had reached Primary 6, Evie had learned some unusual, but irrefutable, facts. It was a fact that all snails were heading for Jerusalem. It was their life's purpose, for reasons unspecified and best left unquestioned. And should one chance upon two snails crawling in diametrically opposite directions, as Paddy Tohill had once claimed he had, then one snail was simply taking the scenic route to Christendom. It was also a fact that girls shouldn't whistle, because it made Our Lady cry, and for every five minutes you laughed, you would cry for ten.

And if a bishop – like Bishop O'Carolan, Mrs O'Carolan's brother – came to stay while his housekeeper was on holiday, for breakfast he liked his egg poached, his bacon grilled and his sausage fried. It was a trial. A severe one for Mrs O'Carolan, Evie reckoned, since her staple diet consisted of cough pastilles, black coffee and untipped cigarettes – which she smoked constantly, in defiance of any legislation. But then her brother *was* a bishop. And he fundraised tirelessly for the black babies.

Evie was in love with the white doctor on the Church of Ireland mission box. She dreamed of one day being the blonde-haired, crisply uniformed nurse on the side of the box who practised efficient kindness on the wards of the mission hospital and nursed countless orphans back to health. Together she and the doctor would cater for the babies' physical and spiritual welfare before going on to raise a family of their own, perhaps founding a small school out in the African bush.

The Fundamentalists, she knew, prayed for their cousins in the Commonwealth and that was that. There was no scope for weaving dreams.

* * * *

Monday did not usually have much to recommend it. After two welcome days' respite from the claustrophobia of the classroom, Mrs O'Carolan did not cope well with enforced confinement, with the sounds and smells of three classes of apathetic children within the one small room. Eruptions of violence could be triggered by the slightest misdemeanour: the ill-timed cough, the nauseating smell of milk warmed to curdling point on the radiators. But for the children, if it was your turn to wash out the milk bottles, peel off the punctured remains of the caps and add them to the silver foil collection for the blind and deliver the slops of milk to the caretaker's cat, the combination was as good as a holiday, even if you sliced open a finger on the unwieldy foil bottle tops

This particular Monday, there was a fresh pile of *Far East* magazines on her desk. Distribution of these round the village would guarantee an afternoon's respite for the chosen emissaries. Evie would be among them. Mrs O'Carolan reckoned it would be churlish to discriminate against her on the grounds of religion, or lack of it, and besides, Evie was reliable, trustworthy and articulate – qualities lacking in more than a few of the teacher's flock. And her parents seemed not to mind.

Unexpectedly, Mrs O'Carolan was in teasing mood. The classes shuffled nervously as she asked them to guess the surprise on her desk. No, not the magazines, that was too obvious. It was the typewritten sheet of white paper which contained details of the first-ever Cardinal Conway Essay Prize. Each school in the diocese was to submit one entry. This pupil would receive a small prize; the overall winner would have their story published and bring great glory to their school.

Wouldn't it be marvellous if a wee country school could win it?

Wouldn't it just, they agreed, and Mrs O'Carolan needed no encouragement to give them a long talk on the subject of the essay:

the cardinal himself, his vocation, his inauguration, his people, his cathedral city.

Evie listened intently. English was her best and favourite subject, with drama and religion a close second. The two blended together seamlessly in her mind: the richness of language, the vestments, the ceremony, the sense of theatre and history. She loved the mystical ritual, the inexplicable sense of the eternal, the sheer loveliness of the First Holy Communion dress that was forever denied her in exchange, it seemed, for being part of a smaller family with a bit more money to go round.

Her talk completed, Mrs O'Carolan instructed them all to begin writing, but to work in complete silence or their entry would not be submitted.

* * * *

Nearing lunchtime, Mrs O'Carolan approached Evie.

'How many pages have you done?' It was almost a rhetorical question. She knew that Evie would deliver the required standard.

'I'm on my sixth, Miss. I've nearly finished.'

'Six pages!' Mary O'Carolan virtually crowed. It would be six good, quality pages, too. 'Six pages, class! And some of you who are at Mass every Sunday in life can only manage the front and back of a single sheet. Ten minutes more.'

Evie put down her pen. She had saved her best sentence for last: the cardinal's imagined thoughts as he observed his red hat at his inauguration, knowing that the next time it adorned his person in public would be when it was placed on his coffin as he was carried to his place of rest. The essay was a gift to her; for Evie, storytelling was the natural way to escape from boredom and pain and disappointment.

* * * *

'You'll win it. You're a cert,' Evie's best friend Lil said as they lay stretched out in the afternoon sun in the middle of the brae, pressing their legs into the warm tarmac surface so it would leave spotted patterns on their calves and thighs. The envelope containing the money for the *Far East* magazines and the list of recipients, marked with a tick where they had paid, lay between them.

'Do you think so?'

'I know so. Stop fishing. Miss will love you forever. Well, near enough. If you were a Catholic, she'd get you beatified.'

'Friday will tell its own tale.' But inside, Evie knew hers would be the best. In the school, for definite. And maybe in the diocese. There was a real chance. She went over the story line by line in her head, delighting in the better sentences, wishing she could rewrite others. Lil marvelled at her engrossed expression and wondered what it must be like to have brains.

The rest of the class had gone by the time they returned with the money. That had, of course, been their intention: to time it just as Mrs O'Carolan was collecting her things to head home. Unusually, the door was shut. As they approached, the girls could hear a raised voice.

'And what was I supposed to do? She was more than willing to write it—'

'*You* were more than willing for her to write it, you mean, because you knew you would have a winner on your hands.'

'Father Devine,' hissed Lil. 'What's he doing here? He never does the school visits. He hates children.'

'Sshh!' Evie nudged her.

They stood frozen as the priest's voice was raised again. 'No, Mary. It says very clearly on the sheet of rules that in the case of a mixed-tradition primary school, non-Catholic children are to be offered an appropriate alternative from the list attached for the purposes of improving their standard of composition and taking part in the class exercise.'

'Oh, my God,' hissed Lil. 'You were supposed to write about

something else. Oh, no . . . could you do another one . . . at home?'

Evie didn't reply. Cold reality gripped her stomach. It wasn't that she'd written about the wrong thing. She was the wrong writer.

She grabbed a protesting Lil by the wrist and tugged her back down the corridor and round the corner out of sight. 'We'll wait here. And when we hear her coming down the corridor, we'll run up and give her the money as if we've just got back this minute.'

'Why? Aren't you going to say something to her? Tell her you'll write the other one at home—'

'Shut up, Lil! Just shut up! You don't understand.'

The tears were not far away, but Evie would not cry until she got home.

* * * *

They announced the winner on the Friday morning, Mrs O'Carolan and Father Magee with forced smiles flanking a self-satisfied Father Devine. Evie did not even hear them. She was lost in the story she was telling herself about the white doctor and the mission hospital. It was one she saved for special occasions for fear repetition would diminish its power. This version involved a leper colony and the selfless doctor had assumed the heroic qualities of a Father Damian. As he was intoning, in her thoughts at least, the heart-breaking words 'we lepers' – acknowledging that he, too, was affected by the dread disease – and his faithful nursing assistant clutched her hands in piety, Gerard Mc-Chrystal was coming to terms with finding himself the school's representative in the Cardinal Conway Essay Prize. This was on the understanding that he had the rest of the morning to write his entry out again, carefully this time, correct the spellings and omit the inkblots. It seemed to be accepted readily enough that, at diocesan level, his entry would sink without trace. He mumbled a thank you of such incoherence that Mrs O'Carolan felt Father Devine's critical gaze burning into her, but she chose to ignore his reproof.

'Don't let them get to you,' Paddy Tohill whispered as he walked past Evie's desk later that morning. 'Well done on the special prize,' he added.

Evie stared at him, uncomprehending.

* * * *

As they walked out together at lunchtime, Lil looked at Evie in disgust.

'What do you mean you didn't know? You won the special prize. Miss said Father Devine said the standard was so high they decided to award a special prize as well. You got it for your other essay. The one about the visit to the dentist.'

'No, I never.' Evie was nonchalant.

Lil was having none of it.

'Yes, you did. Miss said—'

'It's not your fault, Lil.' Evie knew her tone was condescending. 'But I never. You see, you know that essay about the going to the dentist . . .' she paused for impact, 'I never wrote it. It's like I tried to tell you in the corridor. It wasn't the wrong essay. I was the wrong writer.'

Lace Gloves and Quiet Desperation

THE SISTERS GIRLIE AND CISSIE LIVED AT NUMBER four behind a front door painted in British racing-green gloss with a brass knocker which Girlie could be seen polishing with a small wad of lint from a tin first thing every Saturday morning. Despite this dedication, which blackened both the lint and Girlie's soft white fingers, the only people who ever stopped to rap on their door were Evie and Lil, and sometimes their friend Ronan Brady.

The girls called every day except Sunday to see if the sisters wanted any messages. Evie's mam would call with the occasional cake or tray of scones, and the postman delivered the silk thread and patterns from the prestigious London store Harrods. They had seen it on television at Christmas time, this vast emporium of colour and light and magnificence where the rich paid ridiculous prices for luxuries they could not possibly want or need. People who went to London would go there to buy a quarter of sweets just to get one of the souvenir bags: British racing green with gold lettering.

Evie wondered if that was why the sisters had chosen the colour for their front door for it was sufficiently important to be mentioned at school that Mrs Cissie Middleton had the contract to crochet fine silk glove backs for Harrods. Bundles of intricate crocheted backs were dispatched to London, where other anonymous and skilled fingers would stitch the delicate cobwebs to soft tool-worked leather palms. Harrods had a royal warrant of appointment to supply the Queen of England, and such was Cissie's skill that when she had moved back to her home village from London, some six years before, they had continued to send her the work on a weekly basis.

It fell to the girls to take the parcels of crochet up the steep hill to the Post Office on the Main Street to have them weighed and dispatched by recorded delivery. The receipt was taken back to Cissie as proof of posting in case the glove backs should go astray. The Post Office doubled as the only shop in the village and the girls were often sent with a small note for tea, porridge oats, Marie biscuits and pudding rice, which together seemed to constitute the sisters' staple diet.

Their needs were simple.

Daily, Evie would call for their two tin buckets to fill from the tap behind the row of terraces and carry them back, one in each hand to balance her, the metal handles cutting her palms and the water slopping over her socks and plastic sandals as she tried to make do with one trip and not two. The man two doors down looked after their dry toilet.

Cissie and Girlie. Such ridiculous names for women of indeterminate age, though, on mature reflection, Evie reckoned they had probably been in their late fifties or early sixties when she had run errands for them. They were taken for spinsters, but her mam stressed that their proper titles were Miss Henderson and Mrs Middleton, for Cissie had been married in England. In Epsom, to be precise, near the big hospital where the Irish nurses worked. It was assumed that when her husband died she had decided to return to her home village. The couple had been childless.

It came as no surprise to the children, or indeed anyone in the village, that Girlie Henderson had never married, as she was known to be fiercely independent and to have a quick temper. If a ball went over the wall of their yard, it was pointless to ask Girlie to give it back. She'd retort that she had put it in the range, where it belonged. Cissie would return it, surreptitiously, when her sister was asleep.

It was Cissie who lovingly tended their window box, which was overflowing with pansies and petunias, nasturtiums and Busy Lizzies. Girlie had no time for flowers and advised aspiring gardeners to grow only what they could eat. From time to time, Cissie would confide in the girls that she was sheltering a litter of feral kittens in the back shed. She would swear them to silence, as Girlie would surely want them drowned.

Yet Evie found peace in their company. She enjoyed the times she would sit in the snugness of their back kitchen while the pendulum clock ticked, and Cissie, eyes screwed up in concentration over the intricacies of her crochet, would talk to her about the old days in the village, about their childhood, about school, about Evie's friends and her plans for the future. It was a safe haven and she respected it as such.

* * * *

Evie only discovered that Lil had never been privy to such access when they were invited in to wait one Saturday morning while Cissie wrote out the list of messages from the Post Office. Lil, who had never been further than the first few feet of lino behind the hall door, hung back as the kitchen door swung open, revealing Girlie seated at a corner of the table, doing the crossword. While Cissie cooked and cleaned and crocheted and earned the few pounds to supplement their savings and Girlie's pension, Girlie kept her mind alert. Or so she claimed. She listened greedily to the radio: news and drama, the Test match, *A Book at Bedtime*; Cissie favoured the music-request programmes. Neither showed the slightest interest in acquiring television.

'I can't go in,' Lil hissed to Evie, hopping from one leg to the other as if she needed the toilet.

'Don't be stupid. I'm allowed,' Evie whispered back, as if that excused everything, which it usually did, for Evie's parents were known to be particular.

'Just don't ask to use their toilet. That's strictly family. It'd be rude.'

Their kitchen was very like Evie's own a few doors away. Terracotta flag floor, cream-coloured range with a kettle and big pot of washing water simmering on top. Cissie kept her quilted satin Chinese sewing box on a little table beside her armchair. Girlie's place was at the corner of the kitchen table nearest the range. The tea things were pushed back into one corner of the oilcloth and before her was spread the paper, an array of pencils and pens, a well-thumbed pocket dictionary, a copy of the *Radio Times* and a stack of library books, each with a paper marker inserted to keep her place. Neatly stacked to one side of the oilcloth were a pot of rhubarb-and-ginger jam, a yellow china butter dish and half a cake of fresh, floury soda wrapped in a spotless blue-and-white checked tea cloth. The effect was surprisingly homely.

Cissie frowned as she sucked the end of a stub of pencil. 'There was something else I had to get,' she mused. 'Now, what was it?'

Girlie ignored her. 'White flower common in bridal bouquets, starting with G.'

Parallel conversations could be the norm rather than a studied reproof.

'Lemon juice. And vanilla essence, if he has it. I'm going to bake this afternoon,' Cissie continued. Then, looking at Girlie, 'Geranium.'

'Geranium doesn't have ten letters. And when did you ever see a bride walking down the aisle with a pot of geraniums clutched to her bosom? Mind you, it'd be no more ridiculous than some of the things you hear of nowadays,' Girlie chided her sister. 'Come on, you're the gardener.'

Cissie handed Lil and Evie the list and the money. 'There you go, girls, and don't forget the receipt for the postage. There should be a few pence left over for sweets.' She turned her attention to her sister. 'You didn't say ten letters. You just said it started with G.'

'Thank you, Mrs Middleton.'

'Thank you,' echoed Lil. Then, as they were skipping out into the hall, she added brightly, 'Gentian.'

'What?'

'It's a flower. It has a perfume. Gentian violet. My granny has a wee bottle of it in her dressing-table drawer.' Lil didn't know whether to be delighted or embarrassed at her cleverness.

Evie looked at first doubtful, then impressed.

'It doesn't sound like it has ten letters, but it's a good guess. How do you spell it?'

Lil shrugged. 'I don't know. I just remember playing with it when I was wee. It was a dark-blue bottle and she had another wee one that was browny coloured called Californian Poppy. I could never get the wee rubber stopper out to smell it. I tried to with my teeth once, but the taste was putrid. I was just thinking about old women and their bits and pieces. Like wee grannies. They always look happy walking down the street once their husbands are dead and their children are grown up and they have no-one to look after any more so they go to Mass and the shops and the bingo and they always carry wee bags of sweets in their handbag to give out to the children.'

Lil smiled at this imagined memory. Evie studied her face. She was serious. What kind of eleven-year-old girl dreamed about becoming a wee granny and dabbing her wrists with gentian violet?

'Hold on,' Evie remembered. 'Gentian violet isn't a perfume. It's blue stuff you put on cuts and bruises. We used to keep a bottle of it in the scullery.'

'Oh, right. Race you up the hill,' and Lil kicked up her heels and ran ahead of Evie in her lopsided, lolling fashion. She spat out the cinnamon lozenge that Cissie had given her as a matter of routine. They tasted of floury antiseptic, but it would have been rude to refuse.

* * * *

'Does it not bother you not knowing things? And getting things wrong?' Evie mused as they walked back down together, sucking the vibrant blue colouring out of their frozen tubes of penny drink.

'Like at school? No,' Lil shrugged, unconcerned. 'Why should it? You're going to get slapped anyway, so why worry about it?'

Evie knew Lil's passive acceptance of her life was more a survival mechanism than inept complacency.

'Gypsophila,' Girlie snapped as Cissie ushered them back in. 'Baby's breath. Weedy white stuff that they put in bridal bouquets to let the poor girl know what's ahead of her,' and she cackled the triumphant laugh of one who had chosen to be childless.

With her heavy Aran cardigan buttoned tight over her flat chest, her legs concealed under a brown plaid blanket, short cropped grey hair, sallow skin and National Health glasses, she looked asexual, the antithesis of her childhood name.

Suddenly Lil spoke. 'Why are you called Girlie?'

Evie cringed with embarrassment as she heard Lil's blunt question.

Cissie pretended not to hear her and busied herself with putting away the few groceries the girls had brought back.

'I know you now.' Girlie was triumphant. 'I knew you as soon as I'd seen you close-up. You're Marty Fisher's daughter.'

Lil nodded.

'I knew your granda. Mickey. He was at school with me. He had brains to burn. Pity he never saw fit to use them. All the Fishers had brains to burn,' Girlie continued, 'for all the good it ever did them. Is your da working?'

Lil shook her head. 'He has a bad chest.'

'So. And he smokes, I take it? Well, are you a scholar, then, Lil? Is that why you hang around with young Evie here? She has the brains, all right.' She cackled again.

Evie spoke up, cringing as she did so. 'Lil's working on my history project with me. The one about the mill. The one that you lent me the photos for.' She hoped Lil would either remember about her alleged involvement in what had been largely her own idea or else have the sense to keep quiet.

'Your granda Mickey and I were the best in the class at arithmetic,' Girlie continued, ignoring the proffered topic. 'I could usually beat him, though. That's how I got the job in the mill office, as a bookkeeper. The master recommended me. He said I had a great head for figures. Not like her.' She indicated Cissie who, ever anxious to avoid raised voices or dissent of any form, had retreated into the scullery.

'Now, to answer your question, Miss. I was baptised with my mother's name – Kathleen Mary. But, of course, she was only a young woman, and she was Kathleen Henderson. So I got 'Girlie'. And Girlie I stayed, and nothing I could do about it. She . . .' she pointed again at Cissie's back, 'she was christened Elizabeth after our mother's mother. But she always got Cissie.'

'I never knew Cissie was the same as Elizabeth.' Lil was, for some reason, quite interested in this turn of conversation.

'Half the wee girls round here then were Mary or Margaret or Elizabeth,' Girlie went on, 'so they were Lizzie or Elsie or Betty. Some of them would even have had your name. Lily, Lil.'

'I'm not Elizabeth. I'm Lillian Mary Martina.'

'Pleased to make your acquaintance, Miss Lillian Mary Martina Fisher. Remember me to your granda.'

'He's dead,' Lil said matter-of-factly.

'They all are,' Girlie replied wistfully. 'All except for me. God has forgotten about me.'

* * * *

29

'I can't believe people think she's an auld witch.'

Lil was now a regular, if not daily, visitor to the sisters' kitchen. For the first time, Evie had a genuine partner for a school project; it wasn't just a means of saving Lil from the worst of the teacher's wrath. So far, they had heard stories of the part timers at the mill school who went to school until twelve noon and then worked in the mill for the rest of the day so that they continued to receive some sort of education. The reading rooms, precursor of the mobile library, the incongruous cricket club and field. The shop that exchanged the tokens the women were paid in for milk and bread and coal, rendering them useless currency for the drinker or the gambler of the house. An early form of the welfare system.

'They looked after those poor fools of women who got themselves lumbered with a useless man and a tribe of children.' Girlie poured scorn on the pretty, the feckless, the lovelorn. 'How many has Jamesie Murphy now? Twenty-six? It's ridiculous. And how many Morans? They've had to knock together two houses for them, your father tells me, Evie. It's ridiculous. That foolish woman should report him. Animal behaviour. I say to Cissie, it's a good thing I was born a Presbyterian, for I would surely have fallen out with the pope over birth control.'

Cissie kept her head down during these diatribes, crocheting furiously. Evie and Lil wondered what her husband had been like. David, he had been called. But little was said about him. The occasional mention of his name elicited one of Girlie's more strident and ominous cackles, but that was it. Maybe Cissie still missed him. But she had done right to come home. It would have been lonely over in a big city on her own, crocheting away.

'Get yourself an education and your own job and a wee car and then see what you think about all this romance stuff,' Girlie would advise them. 'Not like her.' She gestured towards Cissie. 'She was always too soft, that's her trouble.'

But Cissie would never rise to her. She would work on at her crochet or sit gazing into the flames flickering round the bars of the grate as the huge enamel pot of washing water simmered and bubbled on top of the range.

'I might, only I'm useless at school and there are no jobs round here and I'm in love with Paddy Tohill,' Lil would explain guilelessly as the old woman shook her head in disappointment. 'Evie will, though. She's smart and she's going to go to the grammar soon and then she'll get a brilliant job and forget all about us—'

'No I won't,' Evie interrupted.

'Don't get upset. You think you won't, but you will. That's the way life is. And you're not in love with anyone, either. So it's well for you,' Lil smiled brightly.

Cissie smiled, too, but wasn't drawn into the debate.

* * * *

As the end of term drew close and Evie laboriously but neatly wrote out the wealth of information they had put together on the history of their mill village while Cissie made strong, sweet tea or crocheted in silent companionship, Girlie entertained them with Gothic tales of passion and misfortune, marriage and betrayal.

There was the elderly farmer up near the border who had taken a young wife to a life of drudgery on the farm and kept her barefoot and hungry, exhausted and broken, cut off from her family and friends, she told them. Then one day he drove his horse and cart to town and told anyone who would listen that she had upped and left him, run off to London, and good riddance to her and all like her. The word was that he had lost his temper, worse than usual, killed her and buried her in the bog behind the farm. For how could the poor woman have run to the end of the lane, never mind across the water, without a penny to her name and only the clothes she stood up in?

Or there was the woman who brought up her daughter in an isolated cottage, keeping themselves to themselves, apart from their one visit to the town each week for their messages. They grew increasingly unkempt and solitary and their cottage more dilapidated until it was reported that they had taken in an indigent labourer to work on the small holding in exchange for food and lodgings. A few months later, the old woman went to the priest to ask him to marry her daughter and the labouring man. The quiet ceremony was duly carried out and the couple and the old woman retired to the cottage. Late that night, the shouting and roaring was heard half a mile away. The cottage door slammed off its hinges and the bridegroom was seen striding off into the night. He was never heard of again. Rumour became fact only after the mother died and the daughter was taken to hospital, where the doctors discovered she had been born a man, and the distraught and confused creature ended her days in the asylum.

* * * *

'A pile of nonsense. Old wives' tales.' Evie's mother was dismissive of the girls' colourful gossip. 'I would have thought more of Miss Henderson. Just because there was no room for marriage and motherhood in her life, she should show her sister a bit of respect. And she should stop filling your heads with rubbish.'

The end of term came and the mill village project was such a success that it was kept on display in the school, with Cissie giving permission for the photographs to remain on permanent loan. Evie was relieved, as Ronan's brother Malachy had dropped one of them and smashed the frame. She and Lil had attempted to glue it together, but it wouldn't hold. It was irreparably damaged.

* * * *

Evie went to the grammar school in the autumn, which meant she had no time to run errands or gather round the range to listen to tales of the past. It was Lil who had been Girlie's chosen audience, anyway. Evie had been growing tired of her and her attitude to the gentle Cissie.

Lil was now helping out in the Post Office shop after school and on Saturdays. She wondered why Cissie didn't collect her widow's pension there. Maybe it was different if you had married an Englishman, she reasoned. She offered to get the sisters a credit book, as a favour, but was told curtly that they always paid in cash and had no need of 'tick'.

* * * *

One November evening, Evie was walking home from the bus stop when, rounding the corner, she saw a car parked outside the sisters' door. This was unusual in itself – unless . . . could it be a doctor? It wasn't Dr Maguire's car, but it could be a locum, she supposed. It was a smart, newish Ford; it looked like a cop car. She walked faster. Surely nothing could have happened to them? Even in the random murderous mentality of 1972, surely no-one, however twisted, could have marked out the sisters as a sectarian target?

There was no ambulance.

As she turned her key in the front door, her mam opened it so she nearly fell forwards into the hall. 'You scared me, Mam! What's going on?'

'Come inside and don't be staring. That's a police car at the sisters'.' Her mother hurried her indoors.

'I saw it. What's wrong? Are they all right?'

Her mam saw the very real fear in Evie's eyes.

'What are we coming to when that's the first thing comes into our heads? Aye, they're all right. Nothing's happened. They're in the house. There's two plain-clothes police in with them. They arrived just before five. I heard them knocking,' she added in reply to Evie's questioning look. 'They sounded like they were going to beat the door down. That's when I thought I'd better take a look out the door.'

'That was neighbourly of you. I *think* that's the word.' Fear made Evie cheeky.

'Don't be so smart, Miss. It could have been anyone at their door.' Then, more gently, 'I know. You do worry. You hear about cases of mistaken identity, all sorts. You wouldn't know what's going on. No,' her mam continued, 'your daddy thinks the police must have news of a death in the family.'

'But there is no-one.'

'There must be. Some far-flung cousin or something.' Her mam was strangely offhand.

'Would that not be a job for the uniformed police?'

'Round here? Maybe not. I don't know. I was just seeing if we had a note of the phone number of the minister at the Manse in case we have to go to the phone box to ring. Your daddy should have it somewhere, he's looking.'

As Evie was eating her tea, a knock came to their own door. Her mam ushered the two detectives into the front room and closed the door on them. Her da joined them. She and her mam sat in the kitchen, in silence, until they heard their goodbyes and the door closing behind them. It could only have been ten minutes later.

Her da came into the kitchen. He looked shaken.

'Who's dead?' Evie blurted out. The fear was now making her gauche, stupid. Fortunately, her parents sensed this and didn't pass any remark.

'No-one's dead, thank God.'

Evie sensed a strangeness in her father's voice. A hint of something held back. 'So I don't need to run to the phone box to get their minister?'

This time her mother answered. 'No, I think the police would do that, anyway.'

'Oh, right.'

She saw her parents exchange glances. Then her father stood up and fixed his gaze on her. 'I'll tell you what's wrong.' Her da was taking a chance on trusting her. 'But mind you,' he warned Evie, 'don't be saying anything to Lil Fisher. Or it'll be all over the village.'

'She hardly ever sees her nowadays, now she's at the grammar,' her mam added unnecessarily as if Evie wasn't there.

Her father took a deep breath and looked at the floor, embarrassed. 'They came with news of Mrs Morrison's husband.'

'But he's dead,' Evie insisted. 'He's been dead for years.'

'No, he's not. He's very much alive and he's just got out of jail. He was a bigamist.'

'What?' Evie couldn't understand. Cissie was a widow. Everyone knew that.

'They found out when she'd been married for twenty-two years,' her father went on, the puzzlement clear in his voice. 'The police turned up at their house in Epsom and arrested him. He had another wife and children up north. Cissie never knew.'

'Poor, poor Cissie,' her mam intoned. 'Always the innocent.'

Her husband's look silenced her. 'It was a long time ago,' he said wearily. 'People change. Divorce wasn't easy if you had no money. So, he was charged and he pleaded guilty. He had no other choice. And there was a pile of other charges, too, like fraud and deception and false identity, and he pleaded guilty to all those, too. Like I said, he's just got out of prison. That's why they had to come and officially inform Cissie. That he's out in the community again.'

'Is he round here?' It was all too confusing for Evie.

'I wouldn't think so. The police said he's in England. I doubt that she'll be hearing from him again.'

'There's no reports of him being violent or anything?' her mother cut in.

Her husband shook his head. 'Nothing like that. Nothing at all.'

'I take it Girlie knows?' Evie already knew the answer. 'I mean, I suppose she always knew he wasn't dead . . . that he was a . . . bigamist?' The new word was strange in her mouth.

'Apparently, Girlie always knew the truth about why she had to come home. I bet she made Cissie's life a misery.' And he left the room, head bowed.

Her mother cut in briskly, making it clear she was having no further discussion. 'Go and check the snib's on the door. That's us in for the night.' She took the dishes into the scullery. 'And say nothing, mind.'

'I won't,' Evie promised, and wondered how she could possibly keep her word.

The snib wasn't on. Her father had forgotten. Evie opened the door to the autumn night and stepped out onto the doorstep. The weak white porch light was on at number four. Evie saw the small, huddled figure of Cissie sitting alone on the top step, crying silently. Silent tears coursed down her pale face as she stared into the middle distance.

Evie stood and watched for a moment. She wanted to run over to comfort Cissie. But she had the grace to allow the older woman her privacy. Her dignity. The comfort of imagined anonymity. Evie slipped back indoors and shut the door firmly behind her, snibbing the latch.

* * * *

Over the next week, and largely through her father's measured 'disclosures', it became common knowledge that the sisters had received news of a bereavement, but it wasn't anyone close so there were to be no sympathy cards or condolences.

Evie's mam would look over towards their house and say it was a pity on Cissie. She was always too good-hearted, too trusting. Not like her sister. Men like that always preyed on the naïve, her mother said. It was a sin. Poor Cissie.

Yet what Evie would remember was a small figure, hunched on the top step, weeping silently, too dignified to look for pity. Evie would wonder if it wasn't better to have loved with such a passion, even to have loved unwisely, rather than to be like Girlie and despise an intensity of feeling that you could never aspire to understand. Except maybe at a distance, through the pages of a library book, or as the solution to a clue in a crossword puzzle.

Paddy Tohill
and the SAS

IT WAS PADDY TOHILL WHO TOLD THEM ABOUT IT. He had seen it on the RTÉ news at his auntie's down in Blaney. No-one in the village got RTÉ, even though they were right on the border; they weren't in a direct line from the transmitter or something. A mountain got in the way. It must be true, he insisted, because it was on the RTÉ news that SAS men were being dropped all over South Armagh. They were living rough, it said. Snatching sleep in improvised hides in rough terrain. Camouflaged. Surviving on wild berries and the odd snared rabbit, a transitory existence flitting through peripheral shadows. Caught in a twilight world constructed from the pages of comic books and the grim reality of guerrilla warfare.

They'd have their work cut out living off the countryside round here, Lil mused. None of them had ever tasted rabbit and all that you were likely to find in the shallows of the muddy tributaries of the Blackwater that snaked across the fields, like the border itself, was gelatinous globs of frogspawn or skinny dark sticklebacks. The sum total of its aquatic life could be brought home in a jam jar. Evie had once found a book in the house about food for free from the hedgerows and they had all looked through it, but it had the same portent of promise unfulfilled as her *Blue Peter* annual. This had proved a bitter disappointment. So many things to make started with an empty cigar box, as if this was something you'd find lying about the house. None of them was sure they had even seen a cigar box. And when they substituted a cardboard Embassy packet, the results ranged from disappointing to disastrous.

Paddy wasn't giving up easily. He waited for his disclosure to impact on the small group sitting on the grass verge and leaning against the crumbling stone wall at the edge of the planting beside the nylon dump. Lil and Evie and Ronan and Ronan's wee brother Malachy.

It was another in the endless drag of summer days spent gathered round this unofficial meeting place for those in the uneasy transit from childhood to adolescence, knowing that the new school term would separate them. Evie was going to the grammar school in the town; Ronan was waiting to hear if the master's appeal of special circumstances had got him into the Brothers. Paddy and Lil would simply move up a class in the village school, waiting to be fourteen and try for the Tech and from there, out of the system altogether.

But for now, they simply sought to pass the days. If it rained, they tried to talk their way into Evie's front room to watch the television and help themselves from her bookshelves. Other days, the girls might see if anyone who had a new wee baby in the house would let them take it out in its pram. There was always someone with a new wee baby in the house. Usually Ronan's mammy. Then they would take the formula bottle and dummy and wheel the infant in its pram down what Paddy said was the village's best feature – the road out of it. It was an old joke, but their teenage years would be defined by the innate knowledge that as sure and certain as Evie and probably Ronan would be heading down that road and not coming back, Lil and Paddy, whatever he might say, would only ever cast fleeting and regretful glances towards a horizon they could neither fathom nor approach. It was simply a fact: most of them would live and die within a ten-mile radius of their birthplace.

'So what are we going to do?' Paddy addressed them all.

Evie suddenly realised that some sort of responsive action was called for. It was her duty to inject some order and purpose into their day and Paddy had thrown her a lifeline. The glory of the telling of the tale had not in itself been enough. She felt Ronan's and Lil's eyes on her, waiting, expecting. Hadn't they all sat mesmerised in front of the telly at night as the Troubles moved ever nearer? The grainy black-and-white images that had made them the focus of the world. Dungannon, Armagh City. Street rioting and barricades. Water cannon and CS gas. Explosions on lonely border roads. Farmers filling in the craters until the Brits gave it up as a bad job.

No, Paddy had said triumphantly, the Brits had brought the war to their doorstep to infiltrate the IRA's very heartland. He had borrowed the phrase from his brother, who was repeating what he'd overheard elsewhere. But even though it was clearly not his own, no-one pulled him on it. He shot Evie a look of quiet gratitude. She was smart and he knew he'd overstepped the credibility mark. They all did, basking in the reflected infamy of the blanket term South Armagh, even if they knew it meant the heartland of Crossmaglen and Forkhill, which were as much a place apart to them as to the British media.

Lil was plaiting and re-plaiting the laces on her gutties. Then she'd start on the sides of her wispy fair hair so it came out wavy. There were permanent dark shadows under her eyes. Angular cheekbones dominated her elfin features. Evie thought she was ethereally beautiful. Evie's mam thought she needed a decent feed and a good night's sleep.

'So what are you saying, Paddy? Like, that we should go out and look for them? Are you wise?' Evie's tone was less than deferential.

'I just mean we should take a look round some night. And if we see anything, sure we know who to pass it on to.'

Evie didn't. Nor, she suspected, did Ronan or Lil, but nor did she doubt for one moment that Paddy did. Nor did she even begin to think of asking at home if she would be allowed to go out wandering the country in the middle of the night. Worse, if her parents heard anything about it, that could well be the end of her hanging round with Paddy and Lil, even in broad daylight.

Ronan piped up, 'Could we not go later on the day?'

Paddy looked at him with contempt. 'They'd be hiding out during the day. They only operate at night. In the dark.'

'And did they tell you all that on RTÉ, too?' Ronan snorted.

Lil cut in. 'I could come, surely, Paddy. The night . . . if you want, like,' she added hesitantly. 'Sure it'd give me something to do, pass the time. Go on, Paddy.'

No-one questioned this. They knew all too well none of Lil's ones would miss her if she stayed out every night for a week.

Lil persevered. 'Go on, Paddy. We could go down to the old mill . . . where your Marie and them ones go.'

'And if they catch us following them, they'll beat the head off us,' Paddy barked back at her.

The skeletal building was a crumbling epitaph to the linen industry that had built their village, housed and fed its people and abandoned them the year Evie and Paddy were born. The 1960s were the age of nylon, drip-dry shirts, brushed pastel sheets that clung to your legs with static. The old mill was now home to rats and rooks, a refuge for young courting couples, teenagers escaping from overcrowded kitchens, too young to have access to any sort of vehicle.

'Go on, Paddy. Please . . .' Lil was practically begging now.

'Jeez, Lil . . . Aye, all right. But don't be letting on about it. Don't be mouthing off letting on it's just you and me. None of that. Right?'

'None of what, Paddy?'

Evie shot her a warning look. Tiredness shadowed Lil's eyes; anaemia traced a delicate lavender pattern inside the lids. The blue of the veins threading the taut white skin across the top of her chest reminded Evie of the picture of Dr Harvey's blood system on the wall behind the science table. Would any boy, touched by her frailty, feel the impulse to trace the delicate spider web of veins with his finger? Not Paddy Tohill, for sure, confidently strutting the street, poised for action – any sort of action – in his brother's outgrown faded denims and scuffed fake-leather bomber jacket, all jutting cheekbones and brushed-back dark hair, piercing eyes and wide mouth that Lil and Evie agreed made him look a bit like a young Mick Jagger. Evie had asked Paddy whether he fancied Lil, but he was dismissive. She was forever scruffy, he pointed out. Like a wain. Her fingers were all blood where she tore at her nails.

If Lil was stupid enough to put it about that Paddy had asked her down the mill at night, disbelief and derision were as inevitable as a falling out among friends. Ronan, sensing the disaster potential, tried to smooth things over. 'I have to mind the house the night, but I could maybe go the morra night when me da's back.'

Malachy, as always, refused to recognise the conversation around him. Never a day's bother with him, his mother was fond of observing. Evie had heard her parents discussing the possibility that he was ESN, special needs. But that carried the implications of a *home*. A special school. Best not to think about it. Lil tried to include the youngster. She leaned across to chuck his chin and Evie caught a reek of clothing that had been slept in. Ronan was right. Poor Lil.

The factory hooter sounded, close enough to hurt their ears, and within seconds the first of the girls in their pink-checked nylon overalls began spilling out into the road, coming towards them. Paddy saw his sister linked on her best friend. He rose to go. 'I have to go up to the house.' As one, they got to their feet and dusted down their clothing. 'I've to get my tea.'

Evie turned in the opposite direction, Ronan trailing Malachy beside her. Lil fell into step behind Paddy to go up the hill to the main street. 'We'll call for you, Evie. We'll see yous later when they're burning the nylon,' Paddy arranged.

* * * *

No-one knew for sure who owned the old mill building. The nylon factory had leased the more modern top mill building through a solicitor's office in Armagh. Like the apple-peeling business had done a few years before that.

Evie and Ronan lived on the same row as the top mill and reckoned the only qualification for industry must be that it created a stench as bad as sour apples and rotting peels and later toxic, burning nylon carried on the breeze to their door day and night. Evie was seven when she found out that the mill manager had hanged himself from the banisters in her house when the mill closed. That was why they'd got the house so easily: no-one else would live in it since. The neighbours had gone in after he was cut down, for he'd had a reputation as a miser. They pulled loose bricks from the walls with their bare fingers and cracked open floorboards to try to find out where he'd hidden his stash of money, because as far as anyone knew, he had no-one to leave it to. But there was no milk churn stuffed with white fivers – as they'd heard was the case in isolated farmhouses – no tin biscuit box buried in the garden. And so, no ticket to America, no miracle for a people destined to put in their life waiting for running water, flush toilets, road resurfacing, an end to the open tips where families emptied their dry toilets every week, where children scrambled up and down unstable stacks of human excrement escaping from thin coatings of ash and cinders. Just the broken promise of the road out, forever beckoning, taunting.

The house was abandoned for the best part of a year until the agent for the mill owners, who had since long gone to England, chanced upon the incoming schoolmaster and his young family looking for an immediate rental. Thus far, the ghost had not troubled them.

The nylon factory had taken over the top mill in the late '60s and created its own subculture of pollution. The offcuts and short ends and the paper and plastic packaging were dumped in a shallow crater at the side of the road leading into the mill, overshadowed by the trees from the planting. The fire burned day and night. During the day, it had a cauldron of smouldering and molten waste at its core, ringed by charred bits of scrap metal and damp boxes that had found their way into the site, hard plastic bobbins that wouldn't burn unless they were at the heart of the bonfire. At six o' clock on a week night, it was piled high with the detritus of the day's industry, then Hughie, the caretaker, would douse the pyre with petrol from the can he kept in the store and throw matches at it until it blazed into life, strange blue and pink, acid-yellow and orange flames jagging skywards and singeing the leaves of the overhanging beeches. Occasionally, in summer, an entire tree would go on fire and he'd be seen, a small, frail figure, frantically beating at the burning trunk with an iron bar or a lump of wood, whatever came to hand. Once the hooter sounded and the factory emptied its young female workforce into the street, Hughie would police his bonfire for maybe another hour, poking and prodding at it, sending out great gushes of ash, sometimes bending to pick up a scorched tin or lump of wet plastic to throw it nearer the heart of the mesmerising flames.

He was no sooner gone than children from the streets would gather round the fire, a primeval source of heat and light, to shelter from the spitting rain under the gloomy overhang of the trees. To smoke or gossip. Someone might have a radio. They liked the charts. Radio One. Seemingly immune to the acrid dark smoke clouds that hung over the fire, the stench of melting nylon that tore at your throat and lungs. An odd time, someone would have a deck of cards and the older boys would play poker. Young lads would dare each other to snatch skeins of burning nylon from the fire and dance with them in the darkness, waving and twirling like some ghastly pagan cheerleader. It was bravado, stupidity, for they had seen how molten nylon clung to the skin and gouged out sores that were then wide-open to infection and scarring. Stupidity, for they could have had all the offcuts they wanted and the machinists could buy the slight seconds for a pittance.

There was hardly a bed in the village that wasn't graced with the latest brushed-nylon fitted and balanced sheets, deep rose pink and baby yellow, azure and lilac. The same applied to the lingerie unit at the back, where those who had the delicacy and expertise to handle the fine stitching, the laces and boning, satin and ribbon trims, could earn good money. Big sisters, aunties and even mothers were known to possess, if not wear, luxury items of lingerie that had fallen victim to a trainee stitcher or an uneven pattern cutter and would otherwise have been consigned to the pyre. Size was irrelevant; appearance was everything. Dolls were known to be dressed in them. Sometimes one of the boys would snatch a few and geg around with them, trying to fit them on the pubescent breasts of their imagined girlfriends, who would squeal and shriek with the giddiness of emerging sexual power. Paddy Tohill had fastened a lacy one around the skinny torso of their mongrel, which had tagged at his heels, rooting and nosing in the gutters for potato peelings or crusts. It had padded round the street for the best part of a day, its cerise pre-formed DD cups dragging in the gutter until his ma put an end to it for shame that people might think it was one of hers.

The council bin-lorries hadn't made it this far, either. It was supposed to be a private road. Another dumping ground; another road out.

* * * *

It was at the old mill that they were gathered as dusk fell when Francie walked by, a thin, dark figure hunched against the wind, his scraggy hound at his heels. He walked quickly, hands shoved in the pockets of his red-and-black checked jacket, eyes fixed on the ground in front of him. Always the incessant muttering from between clenched teeth; he made no gesture or sign of recognition . . . and expected none. They knew he had a can of Jessie dog food stuffed in one pocket and his rollies in the other. Greasy black strands of hair clung to his prematurely wash-boarded forehead, brows furrowed in concentration on the unknown.

And always the litany, chanted, monotone, barely coherent.

Lies. Lies. Lies.

No-one knew what the lies were or who was telling them. Or what they were about. Except that it was clearly personal to Francie from his aggrieved expression, his intermittent expulsion of gobs of phlegm, spat venomously towards the hedgerow.

Paddy Tohill's auntie said she'd heard Francie had been arrested in the Border Campaign of the '50s and held in Gough Barracks, Armagh, where they had tried to break him. Evie's da said that anyone with any wit whatsoever knew that Francie had never been right, born late in life to a single mother and reared by his granny until she died. The doctor had removed him from the deathbed where she had lain for days and there had been talk of an Institution. Nothing came of it and, as he was legally an adult, he was left alone in the ramshackle cottage to live as he saw fit. His only relevant communication with the outside world was his daily visit to the shop, where he kept an order book, for the tin of Jessie and rolling tobacco and, occasionally, a packet of plain biscuits or tea. These constituted the only known forms of nutrition for man and dog alike. Then he headed down the road out of the village till he came upon whichever of the derelict mill buildings he instinctively designated his shelter for the day spent with the dog asleep at his side, smoking and staring into space. And muttering.

Lies.

Sometimes, too, he stayed there all night, lost in a parallel world somewhere between waking and dreaming.

But he wasn't that daft. Francie would know if there were strangers about. Whether he could tell you was another matter.

What point would there be in asking him, Ronan mused. And if he did find lucidity and told, no-one would believe him anyway.

Lies.

'Do you think would the Brits try to recruit someone like Francie as an informer?'

Paddy greeted Lil's suggestion with contempt. 'They're dropping their own boys in. Professionals. Have a bit of wit. What would Francie have to inform about?'

'He's around the place night and day. He sees what goes on. And nobody takes any notice of him.'

'And why's that, Lil? Because he's mental. Right?'

'He might be putting it on. He could be a tout.' She looked round the group. A nod of assent would draw Evie and Ronan into the collusive powers of her imagination. But the implications of the word were too sinister to go unchallenged.

There was a silence.

Ronan spoke first. 'You would know an SAS man if you seen one. And I don't think they live on roll-ups and dog food.'

'How would you know, smart arse? They're not dressed like Action Man, you know.' Lil was dismissive. 'And anyway, when would *you* have seen one, Ronan Brady?'

Evie knew embarrassment was making Lil aggressive. In the early days, the young soldiers would call into the village shop. Hearts and minds. One of them, a young black Cockney, had bought bars of chocolate for Paddy's older sister Marie and her friends and started up a conversation. He told them he'd been with the army in Aden. Marie had asked him if he had ever killed anyone and when he said no, she'd countered with, 'Well, you can't be much good of a soldier, then, can you?' and the girls had gone off laughing, ripping the wrappers off the chocolate and throwing them on the shop floor as they went out.

Soon after, the laughing had stopped. Paddy's brother Dessie had disappeared over the border. Marie told people he'd joined the Irish Army. Ronan had asked which one. Lil's cousins had come back from Kilburn. Things were changing.

Paddy was becoming exasperated. 'Look, all we have to do is keep an eye out for anything strange. We're never off the roads. We'd know if there were strangers about. It has to be true. It was on the RTÉ news.'

Paddy's argument convinced all but Evie, who kept her own counsel. Her mammy had no faith in the veracity of the RTÉ news since she had heard second-hand that they had reported that her da's favourite singer, Jim Reeves, had been found alive, having lost his memory after being presumed dead in a plane crash years earlier. 'Pure nonsense,' she had said. 'You wouldn't need to listen to those boys on RTÉ.' Instinct told Evie this might be perceived as sectarianism, so she said nothing.

'I think I seen it on the news, too, Paddy. I think I did,' Lil said, ever ingratiating herself with her hero.

'You did in your hole. Sure the Radio Rentals man took your TV back ages ago. Everybody knows that.' It was a low blow. Now it was Paddy who had overstepped the mark.

'Paddy . . .' Lil began but couldn't continue.

Evie saw the shame in his face. There was silence. Paddy would have no option now but to take her. He walked on ahead for a few yards, looking at the ground, kicking at the loose stones. 'We'll start the watch when yous three have to go in. All right, Lil?'

'Right, Paddy.'

'Right. Best get yourself a jumper or something. I have my jacket.'

* * * *

'I reckon we should start here.' Lil reached out for Paddy's hand as they left the path and climbed down the banking towards the tangle of overgrown bushes and brambles that shrouded the entrance to the old beetling mill. The three-storey granite edifice had been built just yards from the river, on a rutted path running parallel to the main mill buildings. Its tall windows opened on to the thick chestnut trees that lined the river bank. The last of the rusted metal frames hung askew across empty panes. Here and there, cattle had trampled the undergrowth and left cowpats caked over the nettles and dock.

Stepping inside, a stench of mulching leaves and musty wood mixed with stale urine and wood smoke greeted them. Unidentifiable parts of abandoned machinery rusted away in corners; cloth sacks and wooden beams rotted on the ground. The churned mud of the floor gave way to puddles of murky water and clumps of coarse grass. Broken glass and half-bricks lay inside the window frames. Cans and crisp bags, cigarette packets and butts were strewn about at random.

'This is like somewhere you could hide out.' Paddy let go of Lil's hand and stepped into the dark.

'Where are you going?' Lil was apprehensive.

'You stay there. I'm just going to have a look around.'

'What for?'

'To see if there's any signs that anybody's been here.'

'Like what?'

'Jesus, Lil, how do I know? I'm just looking, right? Do you want to go on home?'

Lil shivered. 'No.'

'Right, then. Just stay there a minute.'

Lil huddled her anorak around her as Paddy disappeared from view. She looked up. The beams were woven with spiders' webs. She caught sight of a decaying bird lying in the corner. A rook. She wondered if there were bats.

Then, from the back room, voices. Getting louder. The scuffle of footsteps picking their way through the debris. Two people. The faint glow of a cigarette. Lil shrank into the corner and tried to make herself invisible.

Come back, Paddy. Hurry up. Please.

A stifled giggle, then a burst of laughter. All went quiet again.

Paddy, hurry up, she willed.

Then a crash and a shriek. A woman's shriek. 'What the—! Jesus, you scared the frigging life out of us. What in the name of God are you doing here?'

A thin beam of moonlight illuminated a pitiful tableau. Marie Tohill, her blouse lying open and her jeans undone, clutching a can of Harp. And Denny Keenan, who was clutching Paddy by the scruff of the neck, screaming, 'You fucking wee pervert. You followed us down here. Didn't you? Didn't you?'

'Denny, leave him—' Marie cried out.

'Why? Wee bastard. Snooping about in the dark. What were you hoping to find, then? Come on—'

'We were looking for the SAS men,' Paddy gulped.

Denny relaxed his grip and Paddy fell forwards onto the floor as Lil stepped out of the shadows and the moonlight caught her frightened face. She pleaded with him: 'Denny, we weren't spying on yous. Honest to God. We didn't know yous were here.'

Marie paused from tucking her blouse into her waistband to snap at her. 'Jesus, what age are you, wee girl? You should catch yourself on, Paddy . . .'

A knowing grin spread across Denny's feral face. 'Fair play to you, young Tohill. Fair play to you.' He lifted Paddy to his feet, clapped him between the shoulder blades and proffered the can. Paddy dusted himself down and drank. Denny took the can back. 'Good man. Now, fuck off and find your own corner. And mind you don't get caught. Your ma'd skin ye.'

Lil stood frozen.

'You heard me. Fuck off, the two of yous. Before I lose it with you.' Denny's tone was impatient, his temper legendary.

Paddy grabbed Lil by the elbow and shoved her towards the doorway. 'We weren't doing anything!' she pleaded as Denny's assumption became clear. 'I mean . . . we're not going with each other . . . we're looking for the SAS men Paddy saw on the news.'

Denny laughed out loud. 'That's a good one, Lil. You've a quare imagination.'

Shamed, Paddy grabbed her by the wrist and started to pull her after him.

'It's all right, Lil,' Marie's tone was mocking. 'I'll not tell your ma if you don't . . . unless you have to.'

'But we're not—' Lil began to protest.

Paddy stumbled out through the undergrowth, dragging her behind him. 'Shut up, would you! Shut up!'

'But—'

'I said shut it! You and your bloody SAS men.' Paddy was shamed.

'But you said . . . it was you . . .' Lil continued, frustrated.

Behind them, the sound of laughter. Scornful, older, knowing laughter.

Paddy scrambled up the banking with Lil struggling to keep up, slipping and sliding on the damp grass, catching her foot in the brambles.

'Paddy. Wait! Paddy,' she called after him. He was at the top of the banking, his back turned. 'Paddy—'

'Go on home, Lil.'

'But, Paddy, what about the SAS men?' He began to walk away. She ran after him. 'Paddy, tell them. Tell them we're not going with each other or nothing. Paddy . . .' her sob was lost on his retreating figure. She stood there for a few minutes, alone, shamed, then zipped up her anorak and headed home. At least no-one would have missed her.

Nothing more was said about it.

* * * *

When Lil called for Evie the next day, she told her it had been a waste of time. They wouldn't be going again. Evie was secretly relieved but was aware that her friend was keeping something from her – and that it wasn't good. She fought her natural curiosity. Lil would tell her in her own time.

Paddy was offhand when they saw him in the street. He said he was going away to his auntie's for a while. He wasn't sure when he'd be back.

When Denny passed Lil, he made smart remarks about wee men hiding up trees, which weren't even funny. But then he dumped Marie Tohill for a girl from Blaney and he wasn't around so much anymore.

Lil's ma got her a job in the shop. If anyone asked, she was only helping out, and it paid a pittance. But, she told Evie, it was better than walking the roads all day. She was sorry if that left Evie with Ronan and Malachy, but she was nearly twelve and it was time she got a job. Anyway, Evie and her family would be going away on *holiday*. The word was thick with resentment.

Ronan and Evie walked Malachy round the roads for the next few days, but it wasn't the same. Occasionally, they'd come upon Francie and his dog sheltering in a hedge beside the riverbank or in the doorway of one of the abandoned cottages. Francie never went near the beetling mill. He favoured the open air. Ronan talked of nothing but how the two of them would get away to grammar school in the autumn and with any luck this would be the last summer they would spend tramping in circles round these godforsaken roads to nowhere.

* * * *

By the next year, it had all changed. They were laying off at the nylon factory and it was to close for good the following spring. Ronan's mother stopped having babies and he spent most of the summer in the town with his cousins on his da's side. Two of them were at the college with him. He sent Evie and her family a postcard from Bundoran, where they'd gone on a caravan holiday. Evie took it to mean this meant he wouldn't be about the village anytime soon.

Paddy wasn't about much. Evie's mam supposed he had been going to school in Blaney – officially, at least. He and Dessie seemed to spend most of their time there. Nobody talked much about it.

Lil was working in the shop, and anytime Evie called up with her, she was too busy to talk for more than a couple of minutes. She said you couldn't take your eyes off the wains or they'd be lifting the sweets and, anyway, she wasn't supposed to keep customers waiting. She worked six days a week and on Sundays she went to the pictures in town with some older girls that Evie didn't really know. They went with boys, Lil said, but never in cars.

Around the middle of August, when she was making up the books on a Saturday, it struck Lil that Francie hadn't been in for a week. Then it was two. The owner shrugged and said that everyone knew Francie was as odd as they come; he could have gone off anywhere. Then he stopped ordering in so much of Francie's usual brand of rolling tobacco. Young people preferred Embassy Regal and the older ones Gallaher's Greens, he instructed her as she helped with the stocktaking.

The week they went back to school, the national news reported that a man's body had been found in a field near the South Armagh border. This time it was the BBC who led the speculation: an undercover soldier, an informer, a man on the run?

The helicopters droned overhead; checkpoints sprang up on the labyrinth of border roads. A foot patrol made its way through the village, but the young soldiers did not call into the shop where Lil was stacking shelves after school. The people of the village waited to see if the media pack would arrive to break their tedium, but death was commonplace by then.

They didn't have to wait for the description of the remains as those of a man thought to be in his forties with dark hair, dressed in a red-and-black checked lumberjack jacket. They needed no conspiracy theory. They knew the jacket was shrouding the emaciated remains of Francie, and that detectives would find a tin of dog food in one pocket and a packet of rolling tobacco in the other. The dog had vanished, leaving its owner, dead from exposure, his torment of lies silenced forever by the ineluctable truth of mortality masked across his harmless face.

The Grip of Winter

CHRISTMAS WAS COMING. STIRABOUT SUNDAY HAD been marked in the church calendar and Evie's mother was in a state of agitation. Three times she had tramped Keady's streets and three times she had failed to track down icing sugar. Not even a few elderly packets that had been put to the back of a storeroom, the white powder dried into large lumps inside its pink-and-white cardboard box. Armagh was half-levelled and burned out and she didn't fancy venturing further afield to unknown shopping precincts. She had an acquaintance who went annually to Newry to do her Christmas shopping and would extol its virtues to anyone who would listen, so Evie's mam had asked her to keep an eye out for the elusive white powder. Marzipan, everyone said, was as rare as hens' teeth and black treacle had disappeared off the shelves.

'Them and their bloody co-op mix,' bakers could be heard muttering as they realised the reason for these unaccustomed food shortages. Gelignite was not the explosive of choice along the border; instead, the components were shovelled together in bulk in isolated sheds on unmapped roads to create a notoriously unstable substance that was then transported down rickety tracks and bumpy lanes to its destination.

It was no wonder accidents happened.

The most recent 'accident' had left the community in embarrassed and guilty silence. An elderly bachelor farmer, attracted by who-knew-what salacious image of womanhood, had stopped his bicycle beside a ditch and stooped to pick up a copy of a lads' magazine that had been left there as a lure for some young soldier. His unfortunate intrusion, resulting from the frailty of carnal desire, instantly triggered the attached booby-trapped device. The explosion was heard a mile away by those who had planted it and later cursed their luck. What was left of the deceased was hurriedly collected, sealed in a coffin and buried as soon as was respectable, with the priest, the dead man's spinster sister and his neighbours united in their desire for as little reference as possible to be made to the manner of his passing. The bombers apologised. People hoped it could soon be forgotten. Commentators said, without substance, that it could prove to be a watershed.

In Evie's kitchen, her mother resignedly baked chocolate sandwiches as her seasonal offering for friends and neighbours and said that she supposed the youngsters would prefer them anyway, as few children were fussed on dried fruit. Wartime recipe books were unearthed, the perforated pages coming loose from their wire binding. Substitutes were revisited: semolina and almond essence cooked up in a saucepan for marzipan; caster sugar and water whipped with baking soda over a bowl of hot water to create American frosting. It looked wonderful, thick glossy peaks of snowscape, but tended to collapse into sticky whorls within a few hours.

Presents were mail ordered and wrapped for the plethora of elderly aunts who were, in strictly genealogical terms, distant cousins of her father. But in a family that did not breed well, they served as the extended family required by the season.

The army abandoned their half-hearted attempts to blow up the unapproved border roads and the locals, freed from the weekly chore of filling them in again, concentrated their energy on smuggling washing machines and televisions, toasters and kettles across the border to brighten many a Christmas.

Poitín men arrived late at night delivering their colourless, clear elixir in old lemonade bottles wrapped in newspaper. No money changed hands. At Evie's house, they were exchanged for homemade cakes – Evie's mam's were legendary. Her apologies about the alternative recipes were brushed away in delighted enthusiasm for the finished products. Bottles of Red Biddy, thick and sweet and made from the poitín wash, were left 'for the women of the house'. Evie and Lil knew little of the poitín making except that it was a male preserve and, they would come to realise in later years, was almost exclusively the preserve of those who had no woman in their life. Perhaps it had given tacit recognition to the gay community, offered them a secret meeting place where they would not be disturbed.

Evie loved the stories inspired by the Second World War recipe book and told by her mam who had lived in a girls' hostel, having run away to London during the blitz. The stories were as well loved and familiar as the ornaments that were unwrapped every year and hung on the tree. How the English girls hadn't even known how to make tea and toast. How they had lacked the self-sufficiency of the Irish expatriates. The dances. The airmen, the Poles, the Yanks. How the girls had painted their legs with gravy browning and slept with their hair in pin curls because there was no setting lotion. How they pooled their finery to dress whoever had a date. How heaven was some knitting wool and a new lipstick. Any lipstick.

Evie thought it sounded a sight more enjoyable than the war she was living through, which was just dreary, depressing and cruelly divisive. Increasingly, the girls she met at the grammar and her friends from the village seemed to belong not just to different religions or different politics but different worlds. Parallel existences, touching only when the community ignited into violence. She was glad there was no almond paste, for she had come to associate that sugary sweet, oily, nutty smell with destruction. It was like the lingering sweetness of cannabis permeating a hotel lounge, or the warm, sweet stench of human flesh redolent of vomit that, years later, she would come to associate forever after with the sunny August hedgerows at Warrenpoint.

Then, as if by some miracle of ritual cleansing, the snow came. Not just the expected flurry of showers, but deep, settled drifts, cloaking the lanes and ditches, hedges and fields, making clear and beautiful the crumbling shambles of mill buildings, sparkling in the pale winter sun across towards the mountains. Deep, silent, purifying. The village was left to itself, suspended in the peace of Advent. There would be no school bus, no breadmen, no postman till it thawed. These were private roads and the council would not send a snowplough or a gritter.

They were surprised by stillness.

* * * *

Evie woke to the sounds of her da rummaging about in the back shed. The grunts of exertion, the clatters of the ramshackle stacks of wood falling round him. The exasperated curse as he hit his head off the low roof. She quickly dressed and scampered down to the kitchen to find her mam with a look of deliberate resignation on her face and, in the middle of the floor, a sledge. The kitchen table and chairs had been pushed up against the wall to make room. Splintered and rotting now, it had been fashioned from an old wooden door with what looked like a dismantled pallet from the mill nailed on for runners. Fraying rope, green stains, and what might well have been mouse droppings. A trail of dirt, dust and paint flakes leading to the back door. And smiling like a delighted child as he wiped it over with a damp rag, her da.

'No school the day.' He stated the obvious.

'Where did that come from?' Evie had no memory of sledging, but then, neither did she have a memory of deep snow.

'It was stacked up at the back of the shed. God knows whose it was, for it's a long time since anyone went sledging from this house. It must have been going for firewood. It's a good job I never took the hatchet to it.'

Her mam cast her eyes heavenwards, indulgent, happy for his boyish enthusiasm, his simplicity.

'Once the lads land down, we'll get her out and see how she goes down the brae.'

Straight into the ditch in splinters, Evie thought but said nothing.

'What makes you say the boys will be down?'

'Once they see the school gates locked, they'll be at the door.'

It was a bizarre but true anomaly that in a village more used to the greyness of routine than spontaneity, older pupils would often gravitate towards the master's house in search of diversion: an impromptu handball tournament, a makeshift game of five-a-side, the banter unrestricted by the defined roles of the classroom. *Who's your money on for the cup, Master? Is there anything we can give you a hand with, Master?*

True enough, her da was still dissolving the cobwebs on the wooden frame when Paddy Tohill and the outreach party arrived. Beaming triumphantly, they displayed their motley collection: a crumpled tin tray, two lids from selection boxes of biscuits, a shovel for digging through snow banks. There was the inevitable hanger-on, Lil, shivering and small and bearing a couple of plastic carrier bags which she insisted would be OK for sliding on. One was already ripped in several places. As yet, she hadn't become annoying enough for anyone to tell her they were useless.

The boys were tactful in their admiration, reassuring in their belief in the sledge's validity.

'It's a good, strong frame, sir. It just needs a wee bit of work.'

'A new plank here. A couple of nails hammered into her. That'll do the job.'

Evie's mother was known to secrete from him all but the simplest of domestic appliances. But his enthusiasm was infectious and common sense did not prevail.

'I'll get our Dessie down, sir,' Paddy suggested. 'He couldn't get away last night because of the weather. He's brave and handy.'

Dessie Tohill had not been seen about for months now. Lil, who had grown bored with the project, brightened up at the mention of his name. 'You never told us, Paddy. You never said your Dessie was coming home.'

'I didn't know, did I?'

'Was it a surprise for your ma?'

Paddy grinned conspiratorially at his cousin Frankie. God help Lil's wit, she did say the most stupid things sometimes. 'You could say that. Aye.'

Frankie giggled.

Lil glared at him.

'Dessie would be the man, all right,' Evie's da cut in. 'He and Eric McKee and Jackie Curran were all great with their hands. Could have made anything.' The master's tone held all the wistfulness of the naturally inept.

'Do you ever hear of Eric, sir?' Paddy asked politely.

'Not this good while. They're living somewhere out near Portadown now.'

This Protestant migration from the border was a subject sore on his heart. There was a sense of boundaries being defined, old territorial claims reinforced. A retreat into the ghettoes. Where a family could pass imperceptibly from being a dynamic minority, even a tolerated and eccentric anomaly to . . . what? To a self-styled community under siege, motivated by fear of change, fear of loss of status, fear of rumour and the unknown. Fear of everything that was not of them and theirs.

Ethnic cleansing was a concept unfamiliar to the young, yet frighteningly immediate for those who had fought and lived through the Second World War – the defining experience of their life, just as the emerging conflict would be for the youngsters Evie's da taught. But looking out on the soft purity of the countryside sparkling in the winter sun, they could have had no way of knowing that an uneasy peace would be traced some three thousand deaths and a generation away.

Eric's father was a former soldier, a man for whom forced unemployment had not been easy. Joining the Ulster Defence Regiment had offered routine, financial security, self-respect, a purpose to his day. He could learn to distance himself from the perceived sectarianism, abuses of power, thuggery. He wanted no part of it, but he knew such episodes had been regrettably inevitable in war.

Despite his own and his family's wishes, it had also meant moving almost overnight to a purpose-built estate in what was termed a 'safer' community. His wife loathed her comfortable three-bedroom semi-detached chalet bungalow with its primrose bathroom, hot and cold water and Economy 7 heating. She detested the neat squares of trimmed lawn with their plastic clothes-dryers and thin wooden fencing. She hated the whispering and simpering neighbours, the twitching lace curtains, the undisguised bigotry. But there was no going back.

When he had a couple of drinks in him, Evie's da would become maudlin, sentimental, wondering with an unworldly innocence why decent people could not just live in peace.

* * * *

Evie's da held the runner steady while Dessie Tohill drilled into the boards.

'The army is suiting you all right, then?' he asked after a while. The real question went unsaid. His weary, pale-blue eyes met Dessie's sharp brown gaze.

'It's all right, sir. It's grand. There you go.' Dessie gently lowered the sledge and hammered the last few nails into place.

'That's her. The job's a good one. Get her out there, lads, before the thaw sets in.' Evie's da was awkward in his appreciation. 'It's a good job. Right enough. Will you have a drink after when the boys . . .'

Dessie shook his head firmly.

'I don't drink, Master. But thanks.'

'You're never a Pioneer?' He was incredulous.

'It goes with the territory, sir. Sure I'll take a cup of tea if there's one going.'

* * * *

As the morning warmed up, the first signs of thaw were evident. The snowy crust on the pine trees softened and blurred and began to come loose and plop to the ground. It shrank to disclose the faded green of the verges. Dogs leapt into drifts and came crashing to earth as the powdery snow collapsed beneath their weight. The boys' fingers stung and burned through their wet mittens as they pulled the sledge back up the brae. Toes throbbed inside the thick rubber of their water boots.

Evie and her mam watched from the front steps as the rickety sledge careered downhill, inevitably heading straight for the ditch. The rudimentary rope steering was hopeless, but the thrill was great. Her da went on the first ride and trudged back up the hill, rubbing his back and laughing like a youngster.

Lil pestered and begged for a go and made the descent clutching on to Paddy, shrieking and screaming as the sledge gathered speed.

Still the boys carried on, up and down the brae, exhausted and exhilarated but unstoppable. The winter sun shone briefly. The fields glistened; the sky deepened to azure. The air rang with laughter. Time was suspended. If only, Evie thought, if only this afternoon could go on and on. If only the grim reality, the ever-encroaching and inevitable sense of disaster, could be kept at some unspecified place in the distance, in the future where it belonged.

Death and suffering and betrayal seemed very far away as her father laughed and her mother handed round mugs of hot chocolate and opened the Christmas biscuits as 'they might as well enjoy them now'.

The milkman made it through at around three o' clock, heavy chains dragging behind his van as he slid on their smooth-worn tracks and slowly edged up the brae. He was met by resounding cheers when he abandoned it halfway up and walked to meet them carrying a plastic crate of milk bottles. The boys ran to help him, delivering them door to door, slipping and sliding up the path to the main street with the bottles clutched to their chest.

As dusk fell, the sledge was carried back through the kitchen, trailing slush and grit and leaving puddles of murky sludge across the flag floor.

School would re-open the next day. The buses might even be on.

None of them would ever go sledging again. The patched wooden sledge would remain propped against the wall at the back of the shed until it was cleared after Evie's father's death.

* * * *

The year 1972 opened with the violence that was to characterise it as one of the most cruel the North had known. During the dark days of early spring, the kitchen radio, which remained permanently tuned to the news, told them that a part-time reservist had been ambushed on his way to work.

Her parents wrote, but no-one from the village attended Joe McKee's funeral with its Union Flag-draped coffin, Scottish piper and the unasked-for Loyalist politicians and senior officers walking in step with the mourners.

No-one was made amenable, but security sources speculated

that his killers must have known him, tracked his movements, had an easy familiarity with his routine.

The year fought on until it was autumn again, unrelieved dark days where murder lurked the length and breadth of the border. Evie would still call into the Post Office on her way home from the bus, laden down with the burdens of schoolwork and the impossible daily transition from one world to another. Lil grew increasingly distant, she felt, with the occasional snide remark about the 'new friends' she knew she would never have and sadly predictable jibes about snobbery. Surely they were groundless? But she knew she could not join Lil hanging round the street corners at night, waiting for nothing to happen. It would be ridiculously futile to plead to be allowed to go dancing with her over the border in Blaney some Sunday night, with nothing but the most tenuous of arrangements for a lift home.

One day, just before Christmas, Lil took Evie aside in an unexpected exchange of confidences. She pulled from her jeans a neatly folded cutting from a Belfast newspaper. It showed the cages at Long Kesh. In one corner, standing apart, staring out into the bleak winter sky, was the unmistakable figure of Dessie Tohill.

'Did you know he'd been lifted?'

'Paddy told me,' Lil lied. And they both knew it was a lie. 'I'm going to write to him, so I am.'

They both knew she wouldn't. And it hurt Lil that Evie knew.

'Paddy says he could get fifteen years, but he never done anything. Bastards.'

* * * *

'I hear they lifted him for Joe McKee's murder . . . amongst other things,' Evie's mother said, the melancholy filling the room.

Evie stared at her father. Drying dishes in the scullery, his face showed only immeasurable hurt.

Studying at the kitchen table, Evie bent further over her books, unsure whether she was meant to have heard. It was never spoken about, directly, in her presence.

But as the first of that winter's snowflakes fell softly outside her bedroom window that night, she could not forget the image of Dessie, lean and dark and proud, looking out through the barbed wire at some unseen future far beyond the bleakness around him. As the snow fell on the compounds, wrapping them in silence for another long night, Evie wondered if he'd ever remember another, gentler snowfall, and the day they all went sledging . . .

A Mother's Love

SHE WOULD BE OUT OF BREATH, CHEEKS AND CALVES marbled red by the wind, strands of greying black hair escaping from the frayed elastic. Seasons came and went and she wore the same dull brown anorak over an indistinguishable array of shapeless jumpers and dark polyester skirts. In the handful of days graced with the epithet of summer, she gave her annual outing to garishly incongruous floral cottons, a throwback to her days in the seaside boarding house.

Mary was always among the first to clock in, punching her card in the machine beside the corrugated-iron roller door that led into the store before the boss, Andrews, had arrived. Numb fingers fumbling among the cluster of keys to undo the padlock, drag back the bolt and flood the dusty gloom of the store with the morning's watery light. She would catch the occasional tiny fluff of dusty feather suspended, sparkling, in space above the dark metallic silence of the graders. Yet still she'd be apologising, gesturing away the offers of a mug of tea. The girls clutched theirs, imbuing feeling into their nerve endings, stepping outside to rasp on what would be their last Marlborough Light before the ten o' clock break. While they were exchanging fragments from last night's television, the hours put in between work ending and work beginning again, Mary already gripped the handle of a big tin bucket in each fist and was away down to the hens. They all knew she would already have done half a day's work around that old farm of hers before she began the three-mile trek over the fields, down laneways thick with cloying mud to the main road that brought her to the village. The younger girls would comment on it, why she could be bothered, at her time of life.

Dragging themselves from a vodka-induced sleep on a Monday, traces of eyeliner and wobbles of mascara smudging their pale faces, hoodies pulled on over their tracksuit bottoms, their daytime pyjamas, they yawned and shivered from a relentless mix of cold, tiredness and hunger. Night starvation, they'd joke. Clutching the bag of crisps and maybe a Lucozade that constituted breakfast, and most probably lunch. Putting in the drag of time between school and motherhood, emigration or marriage in the very place they'd sworn at school they'd never set foot in. Eight o' clock start, minimum wage, fingers frozen off you winter and summer, tramping through the mustard foulness that spilled its diarrhoea off the hen lorry to stand hunched over in that dark warehouse, watching the big rubber suckers drop and plop the warm brown eggs into the grey cardboard trays on the conveyor belt below. Taking your turn in the black box where the light picked out any that were substandard, plucking them off to sell to the local bakeries and school canteens as damaged eggs or 'cracks', as they were known.

Why would you do it, they asked rhetorically. Maybe it was the company, for Mary had neither family nor friends, visitors nor near neighbours, from what they could surmise – not that she said much at work, but at least she was surrounded by familiar faces. It got her out of the house. You'd go mad up in that old shack of a farmhouse, Lil said, with no-one but an old dog or the odd stray cat and the crows overhead to talk to. You'd go clean mad, they agreed. You'd be in St Luke's by Christmas and you'd only be coming out in a box.

At first, they had been wary of her. A woman in her fifties come into their midst, a woman for whom the relentless routine of early starts, minimum wage, off at four on Fridays and eighteen days' holiday a year was not a stopgap or a necessity but a choice. They mistrusted her deference to the boss and the office staff – a throwback to the colonialism of tugging the forelock. They knew it to be true that she had effectively managed a thriving bed-and-breakfast business, presiding over a seasonally changing team of chambermaids, dishwashers and waiting staff. She had been responsible only to the owner and his wife, themselves Irish emigrants, who had treated her as their own. Who, in their childlessness, had wanted her to stay in the Isle of Man. Have a share in the business. It would, they had implied, be hers when they had gone.

She must be been worth a few pound, Lil reckoned. And knowing the kind of Mary, she'd have invested it. She must be lonely, the girls would echo each other when they had nothing else to make conversation about. Surely she could have got a house in the village? It would have been hard to get a more reliable tenant. Andrews would have rented her one any day.

Mary was lonely. But it was her choice. Living on in the old family home was her choice. Mary could have told them that it was not really the company that brought her from the isolation of the tillage fields at the shores of the lough. Rather, it was a sense of purpose; it gave her days an order. A routine. She was imbued with a strong work ethic – Protestant, if you liked – and she smiled to herself at the notion. A notion that Lil and Donna couldn't have spelled, let alone understood, for Mary did not share their world. They talked little, for what was there to talk about? She would never forget the shock on Lil's face when Mary explained that it wasn't that she didn't follow the soaps on television but that there was no electricity in the farmhouse. Her father had never seen the need for it and, to be honest, she didn't, either. It would have been expensive, for they would have had to lay a lot of poles.

But it wasn't just the cost.

How could Mary tell them that when she walked home in the evenings it was often already dark, that she carried a pocket torch and knew every bump and twist of the rutted lanes and paths to the door? That she would lift the key from under the flower pot and unlock the back door which gave onto a room as familiar to her as her own body, and within minutes she would have turned up the stove and lit the oil lamps on the table? That she would sit there in her old armchair that had moulded to her, absorbing the peace until she was at one with the world around her? How hours would slip by . . . she might turn on the radio for a bit of music, or be content to breathe in rhythm with the gentle lapping of the lough water, drifting in and out of thoughts, her stream of consciousness and imagination losing themselves in the deep, velvet layers of the night sky, the infinite glimmer of the stars?

The occasional cry of a bird would wake her the next morning. One of the cats might scratch the door to get the privilege of curling up at her feet or on her lap and they would sit in companionable silence as she abstractedly stroked its fur. She would open the door over the grate and lose her focus in the glowing embers of the fire. There was always a book on the go, though recently she had noticed her eyes straining in the light of the oil lamp. It gave her a dull ache between her eyes, a sense of nausea. Maybe she should get a pair of those £10 reading glasses when next she was in town. In fact, someone could get them for her. Tonia from the office, maybe. They were all much of a muchness from what she had heard.

No, she had no need of the electric. It wasn't like in the guest house where it had been essential to run the washers and tumble driers, dishwashers and vacuums, the big televisions in the residents' lounge. Even when she had first gone there to work, in the late '40s, not to have electricity would have been as unthinkable as having an outside toilet. But here it was uncomplicated and she sometimes felt guilty at being so blessed. Her life suited her fine. She could not tell the girls how she baulked at the tales of their interminable evenings spent smoking in front of the television, waiting for the weekend. *Do you like your life? Is this what you want? What you dreamed of?* She longed to ask them but said nothing for fear it would brand her as a snob. Odd. As a child, she had attracted these adjectives. The pain of them could stay in the past where it belonged. She was wiser now, kept her own counsel.

Ah, well, it was she who was fond of saying it. *What you never had you never missed.* And what did they know of a world beyond the confines of their imagination?

What you never had you never missed.

Mary reckoned that applied to men as well. Lil wasn't so sure. No-one, she reckoned, could have spent all those years in a busy resort with people coming and going without a bit of colour splashing on her canvas. A guest house, too; plenty of holiday makers looking for a fling. And as for the locals, didn't you have to be near enough a millionaire to buy a house there? Mary would have been a right-looking woman in her day, with an air about her, an aloofness that some might find attractive. They could not imagine her doing herself up they agreed as they plucked and squeezed, tinted and primped and tanned ready for a night out. Tall and angular, strong, not heavy. A country girl. Clear, deep blue eyes that could still sparkle when they were focused on infinity and whatever it held in her memories.

Mostly, though, they ignored each other but for the customary pleasantries of the workplace. But respect had grown for them as it had for their aunts and sisters before them. They might speculate about a past, but there were levels of vulgarity that were never touched upon. This was Mary, after all. She deserved her dignity. And she was a worker, all right. She strode up and down the lane to the henhouse, carrying buckets, gathering eggs or occasionally running in swift pursuit of a scraggy battery hen that had made good its escape into the store. It was not hard to imagine her running up and down flights of stairs with piles of freshly laundered sheets warm from the iron and scented with lavender, or maintaining a constant hovering presence between the kitchen and dining room, overseeing plates, making polite conversation – but only when she was called upon. Remembering children's names, routines, tastes. Never drawing attention to herself. She had perfected the art of anonymity.

She sat apart at tea break, with the mug she had brought from home and washed and dried herself, the crumbly wedges of wheaten or soda she had brought in with her spread out on her lap. Maybe a slice of cheese. When the village shop started to sell pre-packed sandwiches, she was genuinely incredulous at what the girls would pay for such a convenience.

They would all have driven past the lane to Mary's farm, hardly noticing the track that twisted its way down to the low cottage by the water. The boss and the lorry men would pass it every time they headed into the maze of unapproved roads that spread like a hairnet over the land border. It could hardly be called a farm as such, for the two irregular fields that remained had lain uncultivated for years and seemed too abstract a landscape of tufted rushes, bog water and stony soil to let out for grazing; there was no feeding in them.

Once, her father had planted drills of seed potatoes. In the absence of a son, she was kept off school during the pratie gathering – backbreaking work that gritted your nails, tore at your fingers and left a chill in your bones that the heat of the range could not dissolve. Back at school, the master would wave her aside as she queued up for the ritual slaps for her absence. What was the point? Hadn't his predecessor told him that all the country children needed was to know their prayers and a basic arithmetic so they could while away their adult life standing by their five-bar gates and counting their cattle in pound notes? There were few notes to count in Mary's home. There were no cattle in their fields. Once, when she was very young, her mother had somehow acquired an orphan calf that was bottle fed, but her father had got rid of it before it was full grown for fear it had already become a pet.

Her mother had a few chickens and Mary would feed them and hunt about for the eggs before setting off on the two-mile walk to school, dreading that in her lanky ungainliness she would drop one and her father would take it out on her mother for the waste. The eggs would be boiled for his breakfast. She took cold potatoes, wrapped in a red-and-white checked tea cloth, to school for her break.

* * * *

Sheets now blew on the line, as spotless as her mother's before her, soft from washing in the rainwater that collected in the slimy, moss-covered barrel under the spouting at the back door. Huge heavy pots of it were kept on the boil on the stove for bathing in the zinc tub in front of the embers, for scrubbing nightly the red flags of the floor that dried almost instantly in the heat of the hearth. Outside, turf was stacked in the lean-to shed. She hadn't entered its depths for years and it was still as her father had abandoned it, stacked with bits of rusted machinery, old fertiliser sacks, rusted buckets, rotting planks. The cats slept there and kept the rats and mice at bay. The turf had not been touched since the parlour fire was lit at her father's solitary wake. Starlings nested in the chimney.

Few driving that border road past the end of the lane would have registered that Mary's kitchen window looked out on a view to delight the heart of any urban estate agent. It caught the watery morning sun as it rose over the lough with its backdrop of rolling hills. It captured the vermilion and purple and gold ribbons of the sunsets. Blasts of white fluffy bog cotton, splashes of violet foxglove, deep-orange montbretia and fiery whin bushes coloured the foreground. The companionable silence was broken only by the birdsong or the swishing of the wind in the rushes. A horn from the road might echo, breaking the stillness. The bark of a neighbour's dog could carry miles across the water.

The lake shore was boggy and treacherous, but Mary knew every footstep of her land. In the spring and summer evenings, she would walk it around dusk, every inch of it. The foxes, badgers and rabbits did not hide themselves from a creature who seemed as much at home there as they were.

Lil and the girls did not know this, for Mary knew there was no point in telling them. It was a world apart. She knew they thought her a bit odd. They wished they could draw her into the story of the years away. Andrews the boss must know something, and maybe Tonia in the office, for it was to Andrews that Mary had come after she had buried her father. He had been unable to hide his surprise when she formally proffered exemplary references that mocked the only job he could offer her: gathering eggs in the henhouse. There would be Saturday work as well, he warned her, and Bank Holidays – chickens took no heed of Christmas – but she had smiled and said neither did the hotel trade and neither did she.

Why, he had wondered, had she not cleared out any few valuables and shut up the ramshackle farmhouse where her father had lived out his last twenty years as a widower, unloved and unloving, put the land up for sale and headed back to the world she had made her own? Surely it must have more to offer her? There was nothing to hold her here.

'You've done your duty, Mary,' he had said simply, and she had smiled again and asked him could she start on the Monday week, as she had to go back to the Isle of Man first to sort out a few things.

But what was there here? A few of the girls' mothers remembered her at the village school, anonymous even then; a big tall girl, lost to them in the natural divide between town and country children.

Her father had been a hard man, it was said. He had come from God knows where to inherit an ancient uncle's farm, bringing with him her mother, a shadow at his side. It had been a late marriage; Mary was an only child, an anomaly on a roll book that included families of twenty-three and twenty-six. They were rarely seen in the village or at Mass. People did not visit.

When she was fourteen, Mary had agreed to her master's request that she should sit the Technical exam and had passed with ease. That summer, she had called briefly at his house clutching a raincoat and the small cardboard suitcase her mother had brought to the farm sixteen years before. Mary had left less than an hour later, grasping a brown envelope which contained a reference and her passage money. It was paid back within months.

Two years later, when she came back to bury her mother, Mary found the letters – spread flat and stored in the pages of the family Bible – that she'd sent every month to the Post Office. They had been carefully delivered to the farmhouse when her father was away in the fields. The five-pound and pound notes they had held had been saved in the base of her mother's jewel box. Her father had found and drunk them on a forty-eight-hour bender over the border before the burial, then renewed his pledge.

Mary did not feel disappointed, for she knew her mother had had no way of spending them and she knew she would not have accepted the offer of a passage over to join her. Her mother knew her duty. She feared he would follow, even though there was no sender's address on the letters. She had burned the envelopes with the tell-tale postmark but could not bear to destroy the letters. They were her secret, her comfort.

Mary had surprised them at the funeral. Dignified in a simple coat that whispered quality, she had paid the expenses in full before returning by plane, no less, from Belfast. She was looking well, people said. Maybe she had a man over there. Better that she had gone than squander another life in that godforsaken place. The letters stopped. A year later, the undertaker was commissioned for a headstone. Mary would not set foot in Ireland again for twenty years.

Bridget and Jamesie had not known what to make of this big, shy, awkward girl when she arrived on their doorstep. The letter from the schoolmaster confirmed what she had said, that she was Annie Nugent's daughter. Annie who had been at the convent in

Monaghan with Bridget all those years ago, Annie who had all but vanished but had somehow kept the address from the Christmas card they had sent the year they had declined the unexpected invitation to the unexpected wedding. It also explained in carefully couched yet uncompromising terms why Mary had come and said she could always contact him should help be needed.

Childless themselves, they had warmed in time to Mary. She was a hard worker. She learned quickly. She was totally honest and trustworthy. Dependable. Rare enough qualities in the seasonal staff. Soon, she was made housekeeper and within a few years, Bridget could see that she could indulge her ambition of taking it a bit easier, knowing the day-to-day management of the business was in safe hands. By the time Mary was in her mid-twenties, they had retired in all but name and she was running the place, making it the success it was. She spoke little about herself. Her room was neat and tidy, spartan as a nun's cell. She opened savings accounts. On her day off, she went to Mass, took a walk round the shops and occasionally went to the pictures. She joined the library and changed her books every week. And every morning as soon as it was light and she had a chance, she would walk the seafront, looking towards Ireland.

'Stay with us, Mary,' they had pleaded when her mother's funeral drew her home.

And she had been back within the week, with her mother's simple wedding band and watch and a handful of black-and-white photographs of herself as a child taken annually at school, the date chalked on the board as a reminder.

'Stay with us, Mary,' they had urged her when twenties gave way to thirties and she was a comfort in their old age, though they told each other that if she had shown any interest in marriage and motherhood they would not have stood in her way. But it was a closed book. They were her employers and that was how she chose to keep things. Good fences, she would say, made good neighbours. They valued her work and they respected her privacy.

They had hardly felt the need to ask her to stay with them when the word had come from the master's widow that her father was dying. Surely that would mean the last link with Ireland, however tenuous, would be gone. She had a tidy sum saved away, knew they would think favourably in leaving her a share in the business. She must know she would never want for a roof over her head. So when Mary had asked Bridget for a reference, she had been surprised. But she had agreed unquestioningly.

Nothing had prepared her and Jamesie for the return a few days later: the letter of notice, the methodical packing of the two suitcases, one old, one new, that had more than enough space for what she would be taking back. The rest – clothes, a few books, trinkets – could go to the charity shops. Someone might get a turn out of them. The accounts were closed, the money withdrawn to be transferred to the bank near home where she had opened an account the day after the funeral.

'I'll write,' she promised, and they knew it for the lie it was, though the unaccustomed hugs she gave them were genuine as blood. She felt guilty, she said, that she could not repay their kindness; they assured her she had done so, many times over. But why was she leaving? Why now? It remained unasked, unanswered.

Mary could no more have explained to Bridget and Jamesie than she could to the Lils and Donnas and Chrissies who now peopled her working day.

It would have hurt the old couple to try to explain how, even in the warmth and security of their guest house, her heart had yearned for the stillness of her birthright. Her heritage. They would have been shocked at the injustice that burned within her at her exile. The future that had been taken forever from her the night when her mother had been disturbed from sleep and come into her room to find her father grunting and heaving sweat as he gripped her wrists, the weight of his bulky torso pinning her flat to her bed, forcing himself on her as she wept, quietly, ineffectually. As he had done so many nights before in a way she could neither describe nor disclose. It had been stolen, she knew, long before that. It could not be blocked out. She recalled vividly how her mother, a frail wisp of a woman, had dragged him off her, how she had screamed at him that while there would be no more babies from her, Mary could not take her place. She knew her duty. And he would not lay a finger on her child, ever again, she would see to that. She would kill him first. And she had stood there, trembling, while he stuffed his shirt back into his trousers. And before shame could petrify him, he dragged her mother from the room. Mary heard the blows, the shouts, the screams, the banging of the back door. She lay sleepless in the dark and heard through the dividing wall her mother's muffled sobs, gulping and choking with her own tears, their troubled breathing in unison. But she could not go in to her mother. She could not talk about it. Then, or ever.

Her father had been gone the next morning, but her mother said not to worry; he had taken money from behind a brick in the fireplace and gone on a bender. He would be back in a day or two when it ran out. Worse luck. She moved with efficient speed, gathering together Mary's few possessions and packing them in the worn cardboard suitcase she had brought to the farmhouse as a bride. She removed a few pounds from the false bottom of her own mother's jewel box and pressed them into Mary's hand with an address cut from a forgotten Christmas card. Urgently, she told her a story of her friend from the convent in Monaghan, Bridget, who had married and done well for herself, and how she was going to her, and to be a brave girl. She found a pencil and wrote a short note on the cardboard saved from a packet of nylons and told her to go straight to the schoolmaster, Saturday and all though it was. He was an educated man, a good man; he would understand what had to be done. He would keep his own counsel. Now go. She pushed her out the door. Go.

The master had opened the door to the pale, frightened, gangling girl, and when he read the note, he knew what was expected of him. He explained carefully to her how he would drive her to the bus station where she would get the bus for Belfast, where she would change for the boat. He gave her a few more pounds in case she couldn't find the bus and needed a taxi and brushed away her pride by insisting it was a loan that could be paid back once she was settled there. It was, within a few months. In full.

In the days that followed, the master made sure people knew Mary was safe. That she had gone away to work. He soon closed any snide mouths that suggested she'd had to take the Liverpool boat, the thinly veiled euphemism for abortion. He knew it was not true, that there was no baby; there never would be. A mother's courage had seen to that.

He had been a fine man, Mary reflected, and she hoped that, like her mother, the master somehow knew that it had all worked out and that she was back home now, coming into her kingdom. Her mother had given her the gift of leaving, whatever it had cost her, and now by his death her father had, however unwillingly, given her the gift of coming home. She had more than enough money to see out her days, but she would work on. She was used to working; as she said, it put in the day. And after work she was free to walk her land safely now, in peace, to sit by her own range at night, dreaming.

She had a wealth of memories, of stories she'd read or imagined for herself. And now she had the time and space to find her peace in them. To lie alone on the new divan bed the big furniture store in town had delivered, relaxing into the fresh, soft cotton sheets. To enjoy the silence. To know that no-one could disturb it or take it from her ever again.

The dog nuzzled up beside her. He was old now, like herself. Did he realise she was not her father? He had accepted her so readily at the wake, though he had not known her. He moved stiffly, awkward, his eyes clouded. When he died, she would bury him under the beech tree at the end of the yard. She would not replace him. Why would she? For company? She had been on her own for nearly forty years now. How could she be lonely? She had the beauty around her, stillness, peace of mind. She was at ease, where she belonged. And when she died, it could be sold, if any buyer could be found; it mattered little, for there was no-one to leave it to except the countryside around her. It may as well crumble and decay to become part of it.

She smiled wryly as she thought of the girls who pitied her because they believed she knew nothing of men, nothing of motherhood, nothing of life. She would never tell them that by the age of fourteen, her childhood torn from her, she had had enough of men to last her a lifetime. And that for all their experience of family and babies, love and lust, frantic couplings and false promises, she knew, more than any of them, the incomparable strength and selflessness of a mother's love.

The Road Out

EVIE EMERGED FROM THE LABYRINTHINE DARK OF the underground to the sensory assault of light and colour and life that was Carnaby Street. She couldn't believe it: the mystical, mythical street of magazine articles was here, right underneath her feet. And she was walking it, drinking it in, absorbing every sight and smell and sound and committing it to memory. A busker squatted to one side of the hexagonal, multi-coloured slabs, lazily strumming his guitar and humming gently. The sun was warm on her bare arms and legs. *Mr Tambourine Man*. She sang along under her breath.

This microcosm of London breathed life into the world of her imagination. She was sixteen and for the first time she knew the possibility of being transported into a world of impetuous selfishness, where to be young was not a burden. Where every young man with an English accent was not a British soldier. The busker had long, tangled fair hair and weather-beaten skin. He wore faded cord flares and a denim jacket. He smiled at her. She smiled back. She was young and lovely and she had no consciousness of it. No idea.

A year of determination in resisting her mother's natural urge to feed her up, and the accompanying emotional blackmail, had left her fashionably slim. Her hair was long, straight and blonde in the ubiquitous style of the day. Before the holiday, she had taken the bus to Belfast and spent her Saturday-job money on two summer dresses from Etam. One was cream with a floral print, one black with a fine pattern in lilac and white. She had never before had two off-the-peg dresses. After she had bought it, she had seen the cream one advertised in a teen magazine and she felt like she belonged. She was part of this exciting new world and all its possibilities. No longer an onlooker.

She browsed the stalls, inhaling the scent of patchouli and joss as deeply as if it had hallucinogenic powers. And in its way, it was working its magic. She smiled at the incongruity of seeing the Union Flag printed on aprons, matchboxes, model buses, tins of mints. A tribal emblem reduced to a tourist gimmick. She marvelled at the long cheesecloth dresses sprigged with flowers, the rows upon rows of silver earrings and bracelets displayed on black-velvet cards, the proliferation of zodiac memorabilia.

Imagine if on all those tedious monitoring forms you could write neither Catholic nor Protestant but Scorpio. She smiled. Again.

She was intoxicated with the realisation of it all, that Carnaby Street was an actual place, as real as the muddy lanes and crumbling tarmac toads of her native South Armagh. And as accessible. The money in her purse was the promise of a future, the coinage of possibility. Her mind danced with the prospect that you could get up in the morning in one country and go to bed at night in another. A different world. A different life. Could you really just walk away from all the tedium and misery, shrug off the shadow of sudden and untimely death? It seemed too simple. Or would you carry it within you wherever you went, the dark ghost of your inheritance? Your inescapable legacy?

A kaleidoscope of images from her geography book. The plump matrons of Bruges working their snowy lace at the deep-blue waterfront; the misty Venetian canals and walkways haunted by a litany of doomed artists and lovers; the wild horses galloping the Camargue. They were all out there. And more. Waiting. Evie knew suddenly that this was the definition of magic.

Lil always said Evie was the one with the brains, the one who would get the big job and forget all about the rest of them. She had protested bitterly at the unfairness of Lil's judgement. At the unfairness of the possibility that Lil could be right.

That night, she stood at the open window of her hotel bedroom, eating a whole Mars bar, not one that had been cut into slices on instruction to share with her friends and family. Another first, another indulgence. She was right when she had told her parents she would not be afraid to be in a room on her own. Her da had reminded her you could be lonely in a crowd and a capital city could be the loneliest place in the world, but in her youthful exuberance Evie could not begin to understand it.

As the lights shone out over the city teeming with life and noise and energy, she had never felt more included, more part of something vast and eternal. All over the West End, she knew, curtain up would be at eight o' clock and audiences would be drawn into a different world, thanks to the skill of the actors and writers, directors and producers. The magicians of the arts. One day, she would move among them.

Some ten years before, she had stood at a window, looking out over a city at night. The city had been Belfast and they had been staying with a woman she called her aunt, although they both knew she wasn't. And although she would not know it until much later, they were staying there because her father was seriously ill in hospital and her mam had to stay nearby. Her mam had worried she wouldn't settle so far from home.

Evie remembered being unable to sleep, but it was from sheer exhilaration as she watched the rain puddle the pavements into mirrors reflecting the fairy lights of neon signs, the warm glow spilling from pubs and clubs, the window displays in the big department stores, the supermarkets that kept their lights on all night long, even though everyone had gone home. The paced meanderings of couples coming home from a night out, the unsteady footfalls of a drunk, the purposeful stride of shift workers changing at midnight and again at six in the morning. The buses that ran for most of the night, up and down Royal Avenue in a city free from civil unrest. The flashing cold blue light of ambulances wailing up the Falls to the Royal. The impatient horns of taxis. The first milk lorries, fresh milk for the early morning cup of tea welcoming the new day.

Evie loved it all, this twenty-four-hour live performance outside her third-floor bedroom window. She loved the beer bottles abandoned in doorways, the congealed fish-and-chip suppers spilling from the bins, the wet newspaper scudding along the gutter, the windblown black umbrellas abandoned on the pavement like big dead rooks.

Belfast, London. The city was life, in all its decadence and artifice, noise and disillusion, and it would be her life. Soon, in a year, less than a year, she would be taking the road out of the village for ever. She felt excitement pound inside her and she was absolved of guilt by the knowledge that she had not chosen the city – it had chosen her. She imagined herself in a big city, any big city, at twenty, thirty, looking and feeling and sounding and living as she had done in her imagined future. There was no point in telling people. There was nothing to discuss.

Instead, as she stood at her hotel bedroom window and breathed in the warm August night in 1970s London, she wrote her farewell to the grey village street on a page from her notebook and folded it into the back of her wallet. To keep. For her older self to smile at one day.

Evie laughed. Out loud. From the sheer exuberance and optimism of youth. She wanted to cherish the part of her that would be forever sixteen, with everything just beginning, and feeling life, with all its richness and squalor, stirring within her soul. It was her secret, and she hugged it to her, sharing it only with the dark mysterious promise that was the London night.

A Pitying of Doves

EVIE'S MOTHER HAS HER BACK TURNED TO HER, folding freshly washed and ironed clothing and putting it into a black bin liner. She is methodically folding the washing for the man whose life has been hers for the past sixty years and whose body now lies in its Sunday suit in the graveyard of the little border church. Evie would have thrown them in any old way, knotted the bulky plastic sacks and dropped them off at the first charity shop they drove past. But her mother is not like that.

Evie knows she is looking at the future, that her mother will not move to live nearer her but will continue to keep the house as she always has done, a living memorial to the husband who has gone before. On Saturday nights she will wind up his collection of clocks, which will continue to strike the hour, the half and the quarter at different times. She will water his trays of plants in the back yard. She will not have his gift – if he stuck in a twig to support a flower, it took root – but she will do her best. As she has always done.

The radio will stay permanently tuned to the news. The table will be set, the linen mats starched and ironed.

She will wind his watch and keep his gold winged cuff links beside it. Waiting.

Evie sees her mother gently stroking the soft leather of a pair of brogues that have moulded to the knobbly contours of his foot. Her expression tells Evie that she is with her da this afternoon. Evie feels like an intruder, that there is something voyeuristic about being party to this deconstruction and disposal of the trappings of a life.

'I think I'll hold on to these for a while yet.' Her mother is embarrassed, afraid to be thought sentimental. Afraid the young, who will never know what it is to love the same person all their adult life, will think she is losing her grip. In denial. Will she start setting a place for him at the table? Will she still find herself saying 'we' as often as she does now?

'Keep things as long as you want. There's no pressure on you. You'll know yourself when the time is right.' Evie will be guided by her mam. She will offer no opinions, merely affirmations.

'Still, we might as well let somebody get the good out of these. A lot of them were never worn.' Clothes for holidays abroad that she had tactfully deferred for a better offer, a better time, both of them knowing he would not travel again. 'The Saint Vincent's will be glad of them.'

'What about the coats?' Evie is skilled at picking up on moods, the words unsaid.

'Maybe we should leave them for another time? Till the winter comes.'

'I was thinking that myself. They'd be more use then.'

Her mam smiles and Evie knows she has got it right.

'Becky told me I should get my hair cut.'

They are complicit now, mother and daughter.

'Becky should mind her own business. You don't have to go and see any of them anymore, you know. You've done your bit.'

'Still and all, I'll keep in touch. For Daddy.'

As Evie will keep her unspoken pledges. The things that mattered to the two young people who had somehow created from nothing a home full of the warmth and happiness they had never known as children. Her parents. Evie promises there will always be chocolate in the cupboard, a card on Valentine's Day. New clothes at Christmas and all in warm reds and oranges and bright patterns her mam loves, their vibrancy trumping wartime austerity.

She will do all in her power to keep alive the spirit of the romance between the beautiful young Irish runaway and the fiercely academic RAF navigator for whom his childhood home in Ireland was nothing more than a circumstance, not a place nor a people nor a haven.

Of course, they said it would never last. She too young and extrovert and good looking; he too studious and impractical and poor. It would last for more than sixty years.

* * * *

The bags are stacked in the hallway. They have had their supper and washed up. There is too much time now, too little conversation.

'We'll not bother with the crossword tonight.'

'All right, Mam. Maybe tomorrow.'

'Tomorrow.'

The litany of mutual reassurance that they have done everything they need to, that all is right and proper, as he would wish.

'Have we any phone calls to make?' Evie continues.

'No, I don't think so.'

'Becky?' The name prompts them to unite in mutual suspicion and dislike.

'She'll do till tomorrow.'

The bottle of wine is open, but her mam toys with her glass. She will not anaesthetise the enormity of her loss in drink. It would be pointless.

* * * *

'Packie came up the last day. He had a piece cut out of the paper. From years ago. He thought I might like it. They found it when they were clearing out.' She handed Evie the faded cutting. Evie knew her mam was about to ask her if she remembered it but then checked herself, for Evie had not yet been born when they won the cup.

Three young lads, unruly curls, thin hungry faces, dark pools of eyes, gathered around her da. A younger man, already bald, short and strong, a big presence. And a pathetically small, silver-plated cup.

'He was so proud that day.'

Evie had heard the story many, many times before but she loved it anew in the telling. It was a parable for her da's life. How the education board had announced an open sports day in the Mall in Armagh and how her father had known he could put together the best team of young runners in the county. Underfed, congenitally weak, many of them, but keen. Hungry. Disciplined. The training gave them a purpose. A mixture of old RAF PT routines and cross-country. How they had to contrive to get them a proper kit. They had collected old flour bags, bleached them and sewn them into shorts. White vests or singlets. The collection of gutties, scrubbed and painted with the special whitener recommended for college pupils. The journey into the city on the UTA bus. How some of the bigger lads had been made to pay full fare and a couple of wiry adults had passed for concessions. Joan Harrigan, the best runner her da had ever seen, turning up in a pencil skirt and stiletto-heeled shoes because it was what she thought you should wear for a day out. How she'd told the surly steward she would run in her bare feet, kicked off the beloved, borrowed shoes at the starting line, and that was the last the opposition saw of her.

Joan could have been at the Olympics, her da maintained. A great runner. He had met her a few years after she left school, pushing a baby and an infant in a double buggy through the streets of Blaney. Tired and thin, she had hacked her smoker's cough and told him, good humouredly, that she couldn't run for a bus nowadays.

How the city schools had been bitter, jealous of their success. A mill-village school in makeshift kit had no right to beat off all comers. The man who was the overall head of the board had been delighted for them. Packie's grandfather, it would have been, had driven in on his cattle trailer – an event in itself – and borne them home on the back of it in triumph, carrying the little cup aloft as the Main Street resounded to the cheers of their own.

'They showed them. All the big schools with their pretensions and their notions of grandeur. You can't buy talent. They were set to go back the next year and defend the title.' Evie's mother glowed with pride.

This was news to Evie. Surely she could not have forgotten this? 'I thought it only happened the once?'

'Oh, it did,' her mam agreed. 'The big city schools got together and changed the rules so you had to buy an official kit and attend heats and pay entrance fees and all sorts. That ruled it out for us.'

The story of his life: the little man fighting the authorities, the bureaucrats, against the odds; never giving up; railing against miscarriages of justice; tirelessly protesting about a society that values money and status, prejudice and bigotry to the uncompromising and often painful truth.

'What did my da think?'

'He was angry at first,' her mam remembered. 'But I don't think he really cared in the end. He knew he had won. No-one could take away the day they won the cup. Fair and square. Nobody could argue with that. And they brought it back home.'

They sat in companionable silence, each lost in her separate memory.

'Packie would be a second cousin of the Tohills. By marriage.'

Evie nodded. She could neither agree not disagree.

'It was strange there was none of them at the funeral. You can ask Lil when she calls down.'

Evie could not explain how she dreaded meeting Lil, how guilty this made her feel, how she had no idea how and if they could reach across a gap of thirty years and different lives. Any communication they had was sporadic and through her parents; promises, neither meant nor kept, to meet at Christmas when she was down. Evie chose to believe they both preferred to keep it that way.

Please leave me my memories, Lil. Don't come. I want to remember who we were. Not face who we are.

* * * *

'He was a good man, your da. He done a lot for me.' Lil gripped her mug of tea between bony fingers. She had refused a glass of wine, claiming she'd given it up as it did her no favours. Evie joined her as she stood at the door for a smoke. Now they were back in the same front room where they had watched the Troubles advancing in black-and-white on the evening news. Dreamed a future. Lil was still thin, still blonde and pale. Older, of course, but with the same wry philosophical grin that defined her adolescence.

'Mam was saying none of the Tohills was at the funeral,' Evie said, although she was sure Lil was already aware of it.

'There's none of them about now. She's forgetting that. Sure she's getting on a bit. Never worry.'

'Is Dessie still in the States?'

'As far as I know. Boston.'

'Does he ever come home?'

'He can't. There's nobody to come home for anyway.'

Neither of them mentioned Paddy, killed on a summer's evening when paramilitaries detonated a booby-trap device in a car abandoned on a lonely border road. Paddy and two of Lil's cousins had been heading for Blaney. They'd moved into single file to pass it. That, and the cousins' Kilburn accents, sealed their fate as they were mistaken in the dusk for a foot patrol. Paddy, dead at nineteen, mistaken for a squaddie.

Evie thought she'd brighten things up. 'And I hear Ronan's in Geneva now.'

'He done well for himself,' Lil smiled. 'I always said he would. He's working for one of the big banks now. Megabucks.'

'Mam said. She said he called one Christmas . . . a couple of years back.'

'It was sad about his ma. His da was at the funeral, you know, with Rose, and a tribe of her grandchildren. Malachy was there, and I think I saw a couple of the girls, though I would hardly recognise them.'

'How's work?'

'Same as ever. Nothing else for it unless we win the lotto. What about you? I saw a bit about you in the paper. We were passing it round the egg store.'

'Who would have thought it?' Evie heard the crassness in her own tone and cringed. *I'm sorry, Lil. I don't know what to say.*

'I would, for one. I always said you and Ronan would be taking the road out.'

'Good times, Lil.'

'Aye, Evie. We had some good times, right enough.'

Lil finished her tea. There was nothing more to say. Nothing that wasn't better left unsaid.

* * * *

'It's looking well. John says the ground will be settled enough soon to put up the surround.' Evie's mother stands up and surveys her little domain.

They step back from the soft green mound where they have left a box of pansies and primula, vibrant reds and cerise and gold. There will be no glass domes, no white flowers. The small shrub they planted at first to mark the grave has been moved a few yards away and is flourishing in a shady corner beneath a chestnut tree.

Thin sunlight pierces the overcast sky. Night is falling. Doves gather in their cote nearby. The flutter of their wings is soothing, their cooing the lullaby of eternal peace.

A pitying of doves.

'It's getting chilly. It'll be dark soon.'

It is the signal for Evie to walk quietly away and leave them alone together. Her mam and da.

The dark sentinel yew trees accuse the heavens and they answer with the surprise of a small white butterfly that flits over the grave, across the path and lingers over the lychgate before vanishing from sight.

Life is temporary, temporal. We must keep moving on.

Her mother comes up to her and again Evie feels like an intruder.

In the months and years ahead, she knows that others will urge her to force the move. To invest in a granny flat. Make the decision for her. Just as she knows that her mam will live the rest of her life here, on her own terms, in the hills where she belongs. And if she is alone and frail, she is still living how she chooses until the day when she joins her love in this little churchyard, with the wind in the yew trees and the doves and the butterflies and the grey sky overhead. And when she swaddles her in the quiet border clay, Evie knows it is she who must, one day, walk away, alone.